PHILLIP DAVIS

Justice for the Missing

To my wife, Brandy for patiently listening, kindly encouraging, and lovingly supporting all my efforts.

Contents

Preface

This is a work of fiction. Names, characters, businesses, places, events, and incidents are either the products of the author's imagination or used in a fictitious manner. Any resemblance to actual persons, living or dead, or actual events is purely coincidental.

1

Zion National Park

"You know you don't actually have to do this. Don't you, Matt? I mean, there are ways to spend your free time that don't involve hiking through a river."

"I do," Matthew said. "Did you know that not only do I think this is the best way to do it, but I made reservations and got permits in advance?"

"And he paid for it," Dianne added.

Matthew shot Dianne a "whose side are you on anyway?" look, then offered her a smile.

Rick said, "I know lots of rivers you could walk around in and it wouldn't cost you anything. New Hampshire has rivers, doesn't it? If not, there are probably shallow sections of the Charles you could walk around in if you come down for a weekend."

"But the Charles doesn't have views like this," Matthew said.

They had taken a year to plan the trip. Matthew Conrad and Dianne Chambers had saved for this adventure, read about the parks, mapped their route, discussed the details of their travel since their trip to the Smoky Mountains the year before. For Matthew, it was one of the "big trips" of his life and had been made all the sweeter when his oldest friend Rick Minor had agreed to come along. Zion, Bryce Canyon, Capitol Reef, Canyon Lands, and Arches National Parks in one trip. Utah was the only place you could visit five of the most spectacular parks in America in one visit. He'd wanted to take two weeks to do it, but between Dianne's class schedule and Rick dragging his feet over pounding that many miles of trail, he had scaled it back to a week.

They spent the first night of their parks adventure at one of the twelve campsites in "The Narrows" which marked approximately the halfway point of their 16-mile trek. The crimson canyons, the jagged spires, the smell of juniper and sage in the air was everything Matthew had wanted it to be. He had taken fewer pictures than he had expected to, but not for lack of anything to shoot, but because of the abundance of it. Every step was another vista, every bend in the trail opening to another wonder. He knew he would later wish he'd taken more photos, but for now, it was enough just to soak it all in.

"We're halfway," he said to no one in particular as he sipped piping hot herbal tea from an enamel camp mug.

"So, we get to do this again tomorrow?" Rick asked.

"And then again at four other parks," Matt said.

Rick's smile faltered.

"Actually," Matt continued, "This park has the longest and most strenuous hike I have planned out of all five parks."

Dianne added, "It's a 'if you can survive this, you can survive the week' kind of thing."

Matthew stoked the fire with an aspen branch he'd set aside for just that purpose. "Rick, I can recall a time when you would do this with me whenever we had the chance."

"That was before I made enough money I could afford to do other things." Rick clipped the end off a cigar he'd pulled from a leather pouch in one of the pockets of his backpack, lit it with a wooden match, and inhaled deeply.

"I can't believe that amid all this clean air, with that unpolluted smell all around you, you're going to fire one of those up!"

"Dee, this is the best nature has to offer. I assure you, " He waggled the cigar under his nose. "Seriously though, it's not going to bother you, is it?"

Dianne shook her head.

"Matty?" Rick offered a cigar to his friend.

"No, you go right ahead. Just try not to start a forest fire."

Matthew and Rick had been friends most of their lives. They had grown up in Waltham, Massachusetts, gone to grade school together, graduated from high school together, and stayed in touch throughout college despite their divergent paths.

Rick had Boston in his blood. He was a city kind of guy and needed the pace and activity that half a million Bostonians brought with it. So, when they graduated from high school, it had only been natural Rick head into the city. He knew he would find more lucrative work staying in the metro area than Matthew would find where he was going. Matthew, tired of the city, tired of the hustle and press of metropolitan life, had packed up and moved to Dover, New Hampshire, where he could attend the university in nearby Durham.

Their paths rarely crossed, their worlds continuing to diverge as Rick's career in finance and Matthew's academic and outdoorsy passions developed. When they did find the opportunity to get together, they jumped at it, and they squeezed every drop they could from it.

Matthew hadn't expected Rick would make this trip, but his friend had claimed that he owed Matt one after subjecting him to the Boston Harbor booze cruise two years earlier. Matt had been stuck shaking hands with Rick's colleagues and acting as wingman as Rick tried to charm every lady on the boat, getting drunker between each attempt.

Faintly, Matthew could hear the murmur of the Virgin River they'd hiked through that afternoon. He could hear the crackling of the fire and very faintly the crackling of another group of camper's fire, along with the cheerful lilt of a not quite overheard conversation. He smiled to himself and said, "I think it's the quiet. It's quiet and darkness that we can't totally understand until we're in a place like this."

Dianne smiled and nodded, as much to herself as to Matthew. Rick cocked his head and asked, "The noise I understand, but how is the darkness different? Dark is dark, isn't it?"

"Not really, no. I mean, think about nighttime in the city. The sky is dark, but the streets certainly aren't. Even an unlit side street or alley isn't truly dark. You can still make out shapes, colors, maybe read a street sign. Even out where we are in Dover, the woods are awfully dark but not *fully* dark. Out here, when you really look into the night, you realize this is what darkness truly looks like."

"I don't know if that's beautiful or creepy, Matty," Rick said.

"It's a little sad, actually," Dianne said. "We're talking about light pollution. There's so much ambient lighting in our world we don't even notice it. People used to be able to see so many more stars than we can now. The dimmer ones are washed out. We can't focus on them because it isn't dark enough." She pointed up, above the rise of the canyon walls. "We have campfires out here. There are probably a dozen of them spread around, so it still isn't entirely dark but look how many more stars you can see."

Matthew threw his arm around Dianne. They might come at the topic of real darkness from slightly different angles, but the result was the same. That's how it had worked between them since they first met in the university library almost six years prior. Dianne had been working on research for her master's degree and needed help. The librarian had directed her to Matthew because of his knowledge of the academic journals collections and how to navigate the various academic search engines. It took mere minutes before the two became interested in one another.

Dianne was researching the impact of hydraulic fracturing on public lands in the United States. Environmental impacts, though vaguely understood, were not part of Matthew's expertise. Public lands, specifically national parks and state parks around New England were. So it was that deep, connected conversations about the same topic while coming from different directions began.

It wasn't until her third visit when Matthew was fairly sure Dianne had enough research but was still returning to the library when he got up the courage to ask her out for a drink. She declined and suggested coffee, which was a little more Matthew's speed anyway, and they set a date. A couple more coffees, a night out for dinner and cocktails, and a walk-through Bellamy Park later and Matthew and Dianne were "together."

"Well," Rick said, "I need to take a little walk into this darkness, I'm afraid. Where's the flashlight?"

"There's one just inside our tent flap and I think the other one is on the picnic table."

"Thanks," I'll be right back.

"Don't wander too far," Dianne said.

"No chance. I did enough walking today."

"I'm glad he came," Matthew said to Dianne after Rick had walked out of earshot.

"Me too. I know you two don't get to see each other as much as you'd like. It is one heck of a trip to take a Boston-boy on, though."

"You don't think it's too much, do you? He used to hike a lot; not as much as grandpa and me, of course, but enough that he's not a total greenhorn."

"That was a long time ago, hon. I don't think it's too much. Just remember that he is a rookie at this point; all those years gone by. Don't push too hard. I know these hikes are ones you've always wanted to take, but this should be about spending time together too."

"Are you enjoying yourself?"

"Absolutely. It's beautiful here. It's unlike anything I've seen. I write enough about conserving this kind of place without ever actually seeing anything outside the east coast. It's… it's really something."

Matthew smiled and ran his right hand over Dianne's back while in his left he thumbed the smooth wood of his walking stick. "Grandpa would have loved it."

"I know he would have. I'm sure he's glad you brought him with you."

Matt's walking stick had belonged to his grandfather, but it wasn't just the symbolism of it that Dianne was referring to. A couple of years after his grandfather, Cliff, a nature lover, hiker, and sage according to Matt, had passed Matt approached his grandmother about taking his grandfather's ashes to the White Mountains where the late Clifford had loved to hike. Matthew's mother had resisted at first, but they were able to negotiate Matt taking half.

Of that half, Matt had taken a pinch and put it inside a pocket watch, a little like a locket but perhaps more his grandfather's style, and hung the watch from a hole drilled in the top of the walking stick. It was Matthew's desire to bring his grandfather on all the hikes he'd never get to go on. Though he'd never specifically mentioned Utah and was a New Englander through and through, complete with the opinion that there was never any reason to travel outside the northeast, Matthew knew he'd have loved every peak, every canyon, and every panoramic vista they'd seen and would see.

"Rick has been gone a little while, hasn't he?" Dianne asked.

"Well, I'm sure he didn't go far, and it's open enough out here he's not likely to get lost."

"True. Maybe he fell asleep leaning against a tree somewhere. He looked pretty beat."

"If he's not back in a few minutes, I'll go looking for him. Need a refill?" Matthew asked, picking up the pot that sat by the campfire to keep the tea water hot.

"No, thanks. I think once Rick makes it back, I'll turn in. You two can stay up and chat, but I for one need my sleep if I'm going to keep up with you," she said with a grin and a wink.

They sat in silence for a few minutes, staring up at the stars. Matthew sipped at his tea. Dianne rose and filled a plastic tub with hot water from the kettle to wash her face in. Another couple minutes passed and Matthew said, "I'm going to head out in the direction Rick went and see if I can find him. He has been gone a little while now."

"Follow the stink of that cigar!" Dianne called over her shoulder.

* * *

"Rick!" Matthew whisper-shouted, trying to be loud enough his friend could hear him but not so loud as to break the spell of the night or disturb the other campers. "Rick! Where did you go?" There was no answer. Matthew looked over his shoulder to make sure he'd gone in the right direction from the campfire. "Rick!"

There was still no response. Matt walked back in the direction he'd come, turned at a slightly wider angle than Rick had gone in, and walked back out. "Rick! Where did you go?" Still, there was no answer.

Matt walked several paces in either direction and continued to call, the hairs on his neck beginning to stand, and his pulse quickening a little. When there was no answer to another call, and no sign of his friend, Matt returned to camp.

"I can't find him," he said to Dianne.

"You can't find him?"

"No. I walked out in a pretty wide arc from the campfire and I don't see him. He's not hearing me call."

"I guess he could have gotten turned around and headed back in the wrong direction."

"I suppose, but he'd have to have gone a fairly good distance to not hear me calling. Keep the fire stoked. I'm going to grab the other flashlight and head out in another direction. Holler if he comes back this way."

"You got it."

Matthew grabbed the flashlight from inside the tent and it occurred to him that in this kind of darkness he should have been able to see Rick's flashlight even if he couldn't see the man. As much as he was trying not to, he started worrying.

Instead of leaving the campsite at twelve o'clock, Matt walked away from it at three o'clock, sweeping his flashlight back and forth, carving up the darkness. "Rick!" He called every few paces. There was no light and there was no scent of the cigar. At roughly a hundred yards, Matt turned and walked the same distance to the left, turned back, and walked it again to the right. He then returned to where he'd started and headed back to the camp.

"Still nothing."

"I'm sure he's okay. We'd have heard something if there was a problem."

"Like what?"

Dianne regretted that she'd said it, but it was out now, and she had to finish the thought. "If there had been a... wildlife encounter... we'd have heard something, right? A struggle, shouting?"

"Thanks, love. I hadn't thought about that."

"I'm just saying. I'm sure he's fine."

"Keep an eye out."

"Of course."

Matthew turned and left the camp at nine o'clock and walked another hundred yards. The farther he walked, the more his thoughts focused on the fact there was only one more direction to go, and if his friends didn't turn up in that direction, Rick was truly lost, and this became a crisis.

Rick was not along the nine o'clock path, nor was he along the six o'clock path. He walked back to Dianne, shaking his head. "I have no idea. What should we do? Should we go to the other campsites and see if they've seen him?"

"I guess. One of us should stay here though, right?" Dianne asked.

"Maybe. No, if he comes back here, he'll recognize our stuff and stay put. Maybe we can leave him a note saying we went looking for him and to sit tight so he doesn't go looking for us."

Dianne went into the tent and dug a notepad and pen out of her backpack. She jotted a quick note and placed it under the Coleman lantern on the picnic table. The fire might go out without them, but there would be glowing embers and the dimmed lantern to see by when Rick made it back to camp.

Each of the campsites was about fifteen minutes' walk apart, a little longer in the dark. Dianne had suggested they split up, but Matthew didn't want to risk them getting any further separated. So, as they walked, Matt watched one side of the trail while Dianne watched the other. They took turns calling for Rick, but heard nothing in response.

At the first site they visited, the couple there said they hadn't seen anyone but would send Rick back in the right direction if they did. At the next site, the family was asleep, but their coals still burned enough to see there was no one around. The next few sites were all the same. No one had seen anything, or everyone was asleep. One camper, about halfway through visiting the sites, offered to call the park rangers, but Matthew said he would take care of that if Rick wasn't fast asleep in his tent when they returned to camp.

Once they had walked about an hour from the camp and decided Rick couldn't have passed that far without stopping to ask fellow campers where he was, they turned and headed back to their site. They had been careful to note the way as they'd walked. As they approached the camp, they resumed calling for their missing friend and hoped beyond hope to find him sitting by the fire or asleep in his tent. Neither was the case.

Their fire had burned to flickering coals, and the note and lantern lay untouched. "I'm calling the ranger station," Matthew said, digging into his backpack for his cell phone.

"Do you have any bars?"

Matt checked his phone. "One and it's coming and going."

"One is enough."

Matthew swiped the unlock pattern on his phone and dialed. The connection took a moment and the call quality was poor, but it connected.

"911. What's your emergency?"

"Hi. We're in Zion National Park, in The Narrows, and our friend has gone missing."

"Your name, sir?"

After giving the operator all the information he could about where they were located, where they'd looked, how long Rick had been missing, and a complete description of his friend, the operator connected his call to the park rangers' station and Matthew repeated the information.

"He's not a total rookie hiker, but it's been a while. We're from New England. He's used to that environment. I know he was tired and getting sore, but I didn't think he was in any kind of rough shape. He'd only walked away to take a leak. It's been hours now," he told the ranger.

"We'll get rangers out to you right away, sir. You said you're in campsite three?"

"Yes. Right Bench, right up from River Bend."

"Sit tight. You can continue to look, but don't go too far. Keep a light in your campsite, and we suggest one of you remain there in case your friend returns. If he's hurt, he may need first aid treatment."

"How long will it take?"

"To get to you? I'll get rangers and search and rescue mobilized as soon as I hang up. You're a little ways in, so it won't be immediate, but we'll reach you as soon as we can."

"Thank you."

"We'll find your friend, Mr. Conrad. Keep the faith."

9

Matt hung up the phone and said, "They are calling search and rescue. He said I could keep looking but you should stay here in case Rick comes back needing first aid."

"I don't know a lot of first aid."

"I know. I don't know a lot either. Would you rather go? I can stay here."

"No, I'll stay. If he's bleeding when he comes back, I'll stop it with something. If he's limping, I'll make him a cane."

Matthew appreciated Dianne's attempt to make him smile, but the humor was lost on him. He picked the flashlight back up, marked the rest of the clock face around the campfire, and headed out between one and two.

2

Search and Rescue

The ATVs came in first. There were two of them, their engines shredding the quiet of the night. They parked just beyond the campsite where Dianne was waiting. Matthew, having heard the engines a way off, had headed back up the trail to meet them. The first ranger to arrive approached Dianne while the second remained on his ATV watching the trail.

"Ma'am, we're Park Ranger Officers. We were dispatched to this site on a report of a missing person."

"Yes, it's our friend Rick. My boyfriend called it in. He's out looking still. Matt is, I mean. Rick still hasn't turned up."

"We have a description here of roughly six feet tall, average weight and build, short-cropped, dark brown to black hair, brown eyes, last seen in blue jeans, hiking boots, and a gray winter coat."

"Yes, that sounds right. And he was smoking a cigar." The ranger turned to his colleague and gave him a short, two-fingered wave. The second ranger put the all-terrain vehicle back in gear and headed off down the trail.

"He's not leaving, is he?" Dianne asked.

"He's starting the search, doing an immediate area recon while I ask you some questions and we wait on the search and rescue team."

"Oh, okay. I'm sure Matthew is headed back this way. He'd have heard the vehicles."

"Very good. So start at the beginning. Take me back to the last time you

11

saw your friend."

Dianne sat on the picnic bench and explained events from the time Rick walked away from the campfire until they had called 911. She told the ranger about visiting the other sites and about Matthew's radial search from the fire. The ranger asked a few questions for clarification as she spoke, but mostly just listened. As she was wrapping up the story, Matthew arrived.

"Anything? Have you heard anything?" He asked.

"Nothing," Dianne said, shaking her head. "The rangers have arrived. One of them is already out looking. This is officer…"

"Ranger Thompson. Nice to meet you. I'm sorry it's under these circumstances. More rangers are on the way. This far out, some are coming on horseback and a few are making the hike with dogs. Dianne was bringing me up to speed. I'd like to ask you a few questions if you don't mind."

"Questions? I'm sure Dianne told you everything I can tell you."

"Nonetheless, I need to ask you a few things. Your girlfriend might want to take your place looking around. My partner will have the immediate perimeter checked by now and will be visiting the other campers."

"We already did that! I just told you we did that. You need to be looking elsewhere, expanding the search!" Diane said.

"And we'll do that. We have protocols and they are extremely successful."

"Dianne, it's okay," Matthew said, but he sounded to Dianne like he might not believe it. "Why don't you keep looking and I'll answer Officer Thompson's questions."

"Okay," Dianne agreed, a crease in her brow evident despite the shadowy darkness.

"What do you need to ask me?" Matt said to the ranger.

It was the same, "start at the beginning" line of questions that Dianne had answered. Until it wasn't.

Ranger Thompson asked questions that had nothing to do with finding Rick, but rather what Matt's relationship to Rick was, what Dianne's feelings towards his friend were, and if there was anyone who wished Rick harm. They were questions not about someone who had wandered off into the wilderness but questions full of suspicion, questions about foul play.

12

"Are you serious?" Matt asked. "I called you to help me find my best friend and you're questioning me like I'm a suspect in some crime!"

"No one suspects you of anything, Matthew. We just need to have a full picture of what might have happened here tonight."

"The full picture is…" Matthew wanted nothing more than to say that the full picture was his friend was missing and instead of looking for him, park rangers were wasting their time interrogating him after they'd already heard everything they needed to know from Diane.

What he said was, "I understand. I'm just worried about my friend."

Dianne returned, topped off the teapot from a jug they had filled in the river earlier, and set it on a stone near the fire to boil. Ranger Thompson had walked back to his ATV, just out of earshot, and was talking into a walkie-talkie. Matthew was shaking his head and running his fingers through his hair.

"They questioned me like I'm a suspect in a murder investigation, Dianne."

"They what? Why? You're the one who called it in."

"I know. Protocol, I guess. Do you suppose people come out here to murder their friends regularly?"

Thompson returned. "We'll have search and rescue personnel here shortly, including the dogs. We'll need something with your friend's scent on it."

Dianne went into Rick's tent and brought out his backpack. Matt searched on the ground near where his friend had been sitting, looking for the leather cigar case or the nib of the cigar he'd sliced off, but he found neither. Dianne handed Thompson the backpack.

"Thank you," the man said. "Now, we've got this from here. These are trained experts and even better-trained dogs. I want the two of you to remain here. I know sleep is too much to hope for, but get some rest. You'll be able to help more in daylight. I'll be staying nearby in case your friend shows up."

Matt began to protest, but Dianne put her hand on his arm and reminded him the park rangers were experts, and they would find Rick. Matt unzipped the tent. Dianne poured boiling water into two mugs, grabbed tea bags from the table, and they went inside to catch their breath and calm their pounding hearts.

* * *

"Let me do it, please," Matt said.

"Okay sir, but there is a protocol for this too. We don't want to cause panic. We want to assure his mother that the full forces of our search and rescue teams are out looking for her son."

Matthew had not even thought about these phone calls. The very idea that Rick was missing and a pang of rising guilt that it was his fault for talking him into the trip had overwhelmed him. He hadn't considered the need for phone calls to Rick's mother, his employer, or anyone else. According to Ranger Thompson, it was the necessary next step.

They had to verify, Matthew could hardly believe he was being told, that Rick was in fact missing. Apparently, there were cases, recent cases, of people being reported missing who were simply somewhere else; with a mistress or, having gotten lost, found a road and hitched out of town. The latter was possible, though unlikely as far as Matt was concerned, and the former even more so.

"If he had a lady friend somewhere within hiking distance, we would have encouraged her to come along," Dianne told Ranger Thompson, forcing a smile.

Matthew made the uncomfortable phone call to Rick's mother, following a script the ranger had coached him with.

"I'm so sorry, Mrs. Minor. The rangers are doing all they can, and the full search and rescue team is on their way. Dianne and I are sticking around to help. I promise we'll find him. I promise."

Martha Minor said she'd be waiting by the phone.

The rangers then took over making the rest of the necessary phone calls. They contacted friends whose names Rick's mother had supplied, his employer, recent girlfriends, anyone they could reach who Rick might have contacted. They were early morning phone calls given the time difference between the east coast and southwest Utah, but the officers seemed to reach enough people to satisfy their procedure.

Between the phone calls and the questions for Matthew and Dianne, it had taken a few hours to get through this part of the process. The other ATV mounted ranger had circled back to check in twice and was expanding his search. The horseback searchers had arrived, followed shortly by dog teams. They would send a helicopter up at first light.

"We will set searches at choke points; places it's likely your friend would have headed towards. People follow the path of least resistance, so we can pinpoint routes he might have taken with surprising accuracy. Ninety-seven percent of people are found in the first twenty-four hours, most of those in the first twelve. As the clock ticks, we'll add more searchers if we need to. We'd still like you two to stay here in case he makes his way back. A ranger will stay with you in case he needs first aid and so she can radio the rest of us, and we can get him evacuated if needed. Understand?"

"Yes, we understand," Dianne told Thompson.

"I know this is very trying. I know it's hard to just sit tight, but that's what we need to do right now. Let us do our thing. This team is exceptionally good at what they do. We'll find your friend. Any questions?"

"No. Thank you." Matthew had tears in his eyes. He'd cried to Dianne in the tent but had been trying to remain as levelheaded and clear-eyed as he could when talking to the rangers. Dianne, as always, played the part of anchor, rock, and scaffolding that held Matthew together and gave him something to lean against when he needed strength.

Sleepless, scared, and wracked with guilt, Matthew slumped on his camp stool next to the fire. Dianne added a log and stoked the embers. "More tea?" She offered.

"No. Thank you. I think I've had enough tea for tonight."

Dianne sat down next to him, neither of them sure how to pass the time besides watching the horizon for signs of their friend. Dianne held Matthew's hand and listened to his measured breathing. For what might have been half an hour, her partner said nothing.

Then, Matthew rose from his stool, added a few thick branches to the fire, and said, "How does someone just go missing?"

3

The First 24

The helicopter thumped the air as it circled. Ranger Diamante's radio chirped and chattered, and the rumble of ATVs could be heard in the distance. More searchers arrived. More dogs approached, then padded off into the distance with their handlers. The sun climbed into the sky.

Ranger Diamante, Ranger Thompson's replacement, so he could join the search, was not lacking in compassion, but she was business and protocol first. She chatted with Matthew and Dianne, going over much of the same ground her predecessor had. She used the same script to try to calm and reassure.

They passed the twelve-hour mark. Matthew checked in with Rick's mother a couple times, explaining there had been no sign of her son yet and apologizing profusely he had allowed this to happen. She had been gracious and said there was nothing to apologize for. Rick was an adult and no stranger to the wilderness and got himself lost. Neither of them had been able to cross the line in the conversation from Rick being lost to any other potential outcome.

Matthew called his own parents and Dianne called hers to update them on what had become of their vacation. They steeped more tea. They brewed more coffee. And they burned through all the firewood they'd gathered. Neither Matthew nor Dianne were certain what time Rick had wandered off, but the rising sun as beautiful as it was, painting the horizon in a palette of purples and pinks and illuminating the red-rocked peaks and canyon walls with golden light, was a sobering sign of the passage of time.

* * *

Almost all the neighboring campers had stopped by to visit, sharing their concern and promising to keep their eyes open as they hiked. Two of them, the seasoned hikers, familiar with the park, had joined the search as volunteers.

The hours passed. They felt to Matthew like days. His childhood friend, his drinking buddy, his confidant, and the only candidate for best man should he ever get up the courage to propose to Dianne, was missing. He was out there somewhere, over a thousand miles from home, probably injured since they hadn't found him yet, and Matt had brought him here.

He had invited a friend with limited wilderness experience, at least limited in the last decade, on a week-long national parks trip, taken him on a sixteen-mile, moderately strenuous hike, and now he was nowhere to be found. It was a nightmare.

Matthew had seen search and rescue operations in documentaries. He'd read about them in the news. He'd even seen a search in progress once in the Green Mountains, but those were things that happened to other people, not to him, Dianne, or Rick.

First light had given way to a bright, sweet-smelling morning which surrendered to a warm afternoon. Ranger Diamante unpacked a lunch for the three of them, another searcher on his ATV having brought a small cooler in. They ate in silence. Matthew walked to the other campsites, all eleven of them, checking to see if anyone remained, or if any new hikers had settled in, to ask them if they'd seen anything. The afternoon was full in its glory when Officer Thompson returned.

"Matthew, Dianne, I'm afraid we have yet to find any sign of your friend. We've searched the surrounding area and adjoining trails and are maintaining choke points. Rangers have set up a command center set at the trailhead. We will continue searching, but we're not far from the 24-hour mark. You understand we are devoting all available resources?"

It was more statement than question, but Matthew answered anyway. "Yes. We understand."

"What are your plans at this time?" Thompson asked.

"Sorry?" Matt replied.

"Your plans. Are you going to remain here another night should it come to that or would you like us to guide you back to you vehicle? Is there somewhere you need to be?"

Matthew hadn't thought about that. He turned to Dianne with consternation drawn across his brow. "I don't know," he stated flatly. "I guess we hadn't talked about it. I guess we... I think we were hoping we wouldn't have to discuss that. Dianne?"

Dianne pursed her lips and said, "We aren't really equipped for more than one night out here. We'd planned on finishing the hike today, then moving on."

"You were headed to Bryce Canyon?" Thompson asked.

"That's right," Matt said. "We had a hotel booked out that way tonight."

"Did Rick know that? Did he know what hotel it was?"

Dianne was certain they'd gone over this with Thompson late the previous night, but then they'd answered all his questions and a few of Ranger Diamante's more than once. Matt shook his head.

"Yes. He knew where we headed next. Which park, I mean. I don't think he knew the hotel, and he certainly wouldn't have left Zion and try to get there on his own. He knows we'd be looking for him here. He knows we wouldn't leave him."

Saying it aloud was all Matt needed to make the decision. "We're staying here if that's all right with you," he said, turning to Dianne. "We can get by one more night. If he doesn't turn up before that, we ought to stay here in case he finds his way back."

Dianne nodded. Ranger Thompson nodded too. His expression was stoic, but his eyes told Matt that Rick was not likely to simply wander back.

"Statistically, we are making certain assumptions at this point," Thompson said. "This area is not densely forested. Being lost in the woods is not a likely scenario. There are potential fall hazards; waterways, canyons, even some marshland not far from here and since we have not seen your friend in any obvious location, we can say with some certainty he is likely injured, maybe just a sprain of some other minor injury that is keeping him immobile. He may have sought shelter and fallen asleep or lost consciousness if he sustained a serious enough injury. There is also the possibility of a wildlife encounter, although we have seen no sign and the dogs have not picked up anything which points in that direction."

"What happens next?" Matt asked, feeling unsteady over the direction the conversation was heading.

"Well, as I told you earlier, we find most people within the first 24 hours. We still have several hours to go before we reach that mark, and we are adding volunteers all the time until-"

"And after that mark?" Matthew interrupted.

"We will continue to search, but we need to look at probabilities. We consider the terrain, the weather, the missing person's age, experience, fitness, etc. Then we decide on how best to allocate resources."

Dianne took Matt's hand, sensing the tension rise in her partner.

"You mean, you use those statistics to decide if it's worth continuing the search?"

"We will continue the search, regardless of the statistics, but our resources are not unlimited. For now, we aren't going to worry about that. For now, we are going to focus on finding your friend."

"He isn't going to worry about it," Matt thought. "I'm not going to be able to do anything else. What were the stats on Rick? How many resources is he worth?"

Matt unzipped the tent flap and lay down atop his sleeping bag. Dianne followed him into the tent and lay with her hand on his chest.

"They'll find him, Matt. They will."

4

The Next 7

It didn't feel right to Matthew, living in a hotel, eating at restaurants, or ordering takeout while his closest friend was somewhere in the wilderness, possibly starving, possibly injured, terrified, and alone.

He had volunteered for search and rescue, and for a couple of days they had made use of his help. After that, the number of volunteers turning up had dwindled. They had pulled resources back from the effort, and it became clear the park rangers were getting ready to "suspend the search."

In Matthew's estimation that meant file in under cold cases and move on with their sincere apologies to Matt, Dianne, and Rick's mother.

Dianne had been right. They were only outfitted for one more night in the backcountry, so they had reluctantly packed up their things and taken a shuttle from the trailhead back to Springdale. Dianne booked them a room and Matthew called the park police to let them know where he and Dianne would be in case something changed.

They took turns showering and cleaning up and crashed into the deep sleep of thorough exhaustion.

It was after noon when they awoke. Dianne was the first to drag herself from the bed, followed by Matthew who always stirred the moment she got up. They stretched, agreed coffee was the priority, and decided they'd need to shop. They had packed for a week's vacation. An extended stay hadn't been in the budget, and they weren't sure how long they would be in Utah.

There were hotel and meal expenses, but they also needed clothes. They had appropriate gear for hiking and camping, and they each had a couple of outfits for their travel days, but if the stay became extended, they didn't want to bother with finding a laundromat. They opted for cheap clothes at the nearest Walmart.

Their first night back in Springdale, dinner was a BLT for Matthew and a veggie wrap for Dianne from a cafe near the hotel. It was over this light, early evening meal they made their plans.

"It sounds like after a week they will close the case, or at least move it to the cold case department," Matthew said.

"I don't think they will give up entirely. I think it just means that based on their statistics and probabilities, they can't justify the resources."

"I know. I just don't understand. I mean, I know there are a lot of canyons out there. There are little caves, hidden spots and corners all over the park he could have hunkered down in. I know it's possible he wandered right out of the park, but there would be some sign, wouldn't there? There would have to be some trace. And with all these people, the helicopter, the dogs... I just don't understand what could have happened to him."

Dianne, secretly, had settled in her mind there had been a wildlife attack. Rick had been killed and dragged off by a bobcat or had gotten injured somewhere and couldn't call for help. She hadn't mentioned this conclusion to Matthew, who was in no way prepared to discuss the fact Rick was gone.

"I know. I don't understand either," she said.

"And I... I understand the resources thing. I do. But I don't understand how they can just call it off. He's a person. He has a life. He's out there somewhere, and they're prepared to give up on him. I can't. I won't."

"Are you going to go back out? Search and rescue said they'd call if they needed volunteers."

"I'm not waiting for them to call. I'm going to keep looking whether it's coordinated with them or not."

Dianne took a deep breath. "For how long? We're more than halfway through the vacation time we took. How long are you planning on staying? I don't know if I can stay past what we'd planned. I don't know, even given the circumstances, my professors will let me miss more class. I can't start them over, Matt. They won't come around until semester after next, and I just can't."

"I know. I wouldn't expect you to. I don't know that the university will grant me any additional time either. Maybe I can add my sick days to the end of the vacation days, but... I don't know. I hope I don't need to." Dianne noted the tremble in his voice and the slight clenching of his jaw which said some part of Matthew was coming to grips with the fact he might have to leave Utah without Rick.

"Do you know where we're going to look next?" Dianne asked. "We've searched a pretty wide area already. The volunteers covered an impressive gird, and the helicopter swept all day for a couple of days. They stationed people at all the routes he was likely to follow if he got lost..."

"Then we look in the unlikely places. You don't have to go if you're too exhausted. I can go out for a while myself."

"Are you going out tonight?" She asked.

"Might as well. I can't just sit here, and there are a few more hours until dark."

* * *

The next two days were very much the same; up at dawn, out until dark, a meal at a Springdale restaurant if they got around to it. They spent the days following trails and hiking off trails. They called Rick's name. They shouted and whistled and did everything search and rescue told them to do when they'd been official volunteers and every unofficial thing they could think of.

Matthew had purchased an over-sized version of the official park map, a trail guide from the visitor's center bookstore, and a pack of highlighters and a ruler from a nearby Walmart. They marked their own grids and highlighted places they'd been. They put checkmarks in places they hadn't been and wanted to explore, then crossed them off once they'd visited. Dianne propped Matt up and added as much levelheaded analysis as she could while her partner vacillated between his own characteristic levelheadedness and a kind of manic scatter.

They had arrived in Springdale on Saturday, explored the town a little, visited the Zion visitor's center, and had a delightful meal at a nearby steakhouse. Sunday was the hike into The Narrows, and Sunday night had been the night Rick went missing. It was now Friday night. They had a flight out of Cedar City Sunday morning.

They hadn't re-opened the discussion since their first night back in Springdale about what happened Sunday if they hadn't found Rick by Saturday night. Dianne knew it was a conversation they needed to have. It had become clear that, though Matt seemed to be adjusting to the possibility they wouldn't find Rick in time, he wasn't leaving.

"Well, where do we look tomorrow?" She asked as an opener.

Matt was sitting on the edge of the hotel bed, phone in one hand, the other at his lips, while he gnawed at his thumbnail.

"Oh, Matt! Please. You know that's disgusting."

He didn't respond, though he did, mechanically, remove his thumbnail from his mouth and instead ran his fingers through his hair.

"Matt?"

"Did you know somewhere between one and two thousand people have gone missing in US national parks?"

"What?"

"Common estimates seem to be around 1,600. No one keeps a list though."

"Matt? What are you reading?"

"I mean, they have a website, the park services. They have a site for cold cases. Rick is already there. They've suspended the search. I guess they hadn't gotten around to telling us."

"I'm so sorry, Matt."

"But there is no master list. There's no... nowhere that lists all the cases, open or closed, and there are so many... just vanished."

"People can't just vanish, Matt. You know that. Something must have happened to them. What does the parks' website say?"

"There's a tip line. There's an annual report from Investigative Services and a description of how they operate, but... but I'm reading in other places they don't have a centralized database for missing person reports. That seems strange. I'm sure they have records of how many mountain lions are in the park or how many ground squirrels, but not missing people."

Dianne knew databases for animals existed, especially for predators or threatened species. She'd accessed them many times as part of her research. It was a database like the one Matt was talking about that had supplied much of the data she used when disseminating information in Pennsylvania about fracking and its effect on local wildlife populations. She found it hard to believe, as Matthew did, no such database existed for people.

"The Department of the Interior must keep something like that, or the Justice Department? I don't know where that would get filed," Dianne said.

"The National Park Service is part of the executive branch. I know that, but I don't know where it goes from there or where missing persons would be nested in the bureaucracy tree. My point is, though, that these people are just *gone*. Searches usually get suspended between seven and fourteen days based on probabilities, and then these people are just gone. Loved ones still look. Some post rewards. Local news might get involved. Some even make national news, but they are just gone. Sometimes remains will turn up. Sometimes the people turn up, in rough shape or a long way from where they were, but the ones that don't... they're just missing."

Dianne sat on the edge of the bed next to Matt and stroked his back. He continued staring at the article open on his phone. "I'm staying, Dianne. I can't stay indefinitely, but I can't leave until I'm sure I've done everything I can. I don't have the money for a reward. I'll talk to Martha about that and see what she wants to do. Maybe Rick's firm will get involved. In the meantime, I have to keep looking."

Dianne bit the inside of her lip then said, "I understand Matt. I do. How much more can you do though? And, I have to get back. I'm sorry, but I do. And you should come back too. We already have the tickets."

"I know. I know you have to go. I wish you didn't. I wish you could stay with me, but I understand. I'll pay for the change of plans for my ticket, and I'll come home soon. Dr. Michaels is going to let me burn up some sick time to stay here, but there's a limit to that too."

"You've already asked him?"

"I emailed him this morning to see what he'd say."

"I see. Matt, if you stay, you can't stay too long. It will just get harder to leave."

"I know. And I have to get back, eventually. I hope you don't mind looking after things for a few days without me."

"I'll be fine. Have you talked to your parents?"

"I checked in with them last night when I went for my walk." Even with a full day of hiking and searching, Matt still went on walks every evening, sometimes every morning too. He was a walker, a hiker through and through. He couldn't sit still even at home. "There's too much to see," he'd once told Dianne, but she suspected there was also too much to think about.

"They're worried. They're upset," Matthew said, "but they understand that I need to stay here a little while longer. I guess they've been talking to Martha too. There's going to be a vigil or something for him at my parents' church."

"In Waltham?"

"Yeah. They asked if we'd come, and I said I was thinking about staying here. I told them you would probably head back soon but would have to get to class so you weren't likely to make it either, but I'm sure they'd appreciate it if you visited at some point."

"I'll wait for you to come home."

"Okay."

"There is one more day. Maybe we'll have a breakthrough tomorrow."

5

The Squirrel

There had been no breakthroughs in the search on Saturday. It had been a somber day spent checking the remaining few places Matt had indicated on their map. They shared a quiet takeout dinner in Springdale that evening. Dianne packed and Matthew laid the park map on the small hotel room table and looked for additional locations to search the next day.

Sunday morning, Matthew drove Dianne to the airport, and they repeated much of the same conversation about going home they'd had twice already. Matt helped Dianne get her bags out of the trunk of the rental and enveloped her in a tight hug.

"Take care of yourself, Matt," Dianne said. "Come home to me soon."

"I will. I love you."

"I love you too," Dianne said, cupping his face in her palm.

As she stepped through the airport's automatic doors, Matt put his hand in his pocket and fingered the little box he'd been carrying there for a week. Zion National Park, or perhaps under one of the grand formations at Arches, maybe sunset in Bryce Canyon; Matt hadn't been sure when or exactly where he would do it, but he had planned on proposing somewhere along this trip. His future best man would be there to witness. It would happen in a gorgeous national park with his grandfather and the glory of nature to share it.

It hadn't been the first time he'd planned on proposing. He had carried the ring with him a year ago when they hiked in the Great Smoky Mountains.

There had been a romantic restaurant in the foothills, a scenic view, a quiet moment, but he hadn't been able to do it.

It wasn't Dianne. It wasn't about commitment, as his mother suggested. It was confidence. There was a nagging feeling when it got right down to the moment to propose that one day Dianne would move on. It might be her career took her away from him. It might be boredom. Something would let her slip through his grasp, and it would only be harder on both if they were engaged, never mind if they were married. He wasn't sure whatever she saw in him would be enough if some opportunity came along which Matt didn't fit into. He had plenty of faith in her. He knew she was loyal, honest, and decent. It was that he lacked certainty he was everything she deserved.

He'd talked to Rick about it on more than one occasion. Even the consummate bachelor had encouraged him to "pop the question." When Matt voiced his concerns, Rick had said to "Quit being a dumbass. She loves you." And he probably was being a dumbass. That's why he would try again this trip. And then Rick went missing. The thick of a search and rescue operation for your best friend, surrounded by park services personnel and search and rescue sporting reflective vests, wasn't really the time.

Matthew's mother has entered the "when are you going to give me grandkids," stage of motherhood. His father left it well enough alone. He was preoccupied with being disappointed in Matthew's career choices.

Grandma Rose, though, she got it. "You do it when you're ready to do it. Or you don't." Grandma Rose had always been like that, no pressure, no expectations. After Grandpa Cliff had passed, and she moved in with Matt's parents, Matt and Rose had become closer than ever, leaning on each other to help heal the wounds of Grandpa Cliff's passing. She knew there had been a bond between them since Matt was a boy, and Matt knew no two people loved one another the way Rose and Cliff had.

He had spoken to his grandmother two nights ago. After he'd hung up with his father, Grandma Rose called. She didn't play, "pass the cell phone" like his parents did. She wanted her own phone call with him and used it as an excuse to step onto the porch outside her room and have a nightcap.

"Honey, you do what you have to do. That's all there is to it. Everyone else will be fine. You'll work things out with your job, and if Dianne comes back before you, you'll work that out too. You know your grandfather would have kept looking, don't you? If he was still around, he'd probably be down there helping you right now."

That had been the deciding moment for Matt. It was grandma's words, especially those about his grandpa that sealed the deal. He had to stay in Utah just a little longer.

* * *

It was 10:30 am when Matthew arrived back in Springdale. It was almost noon by the time he'd ridden the shuttle to his destination. Their campsite had been at the far north end of the park, along the West Rim. Search and rescue had started there and worked their way east, west, and north out of the park. They had spent little time looking to the south, not beyond what they considered the most likely routes in that direction. The statistics said he wasn't likely to have gone that way.

Volunteers had spread out, the chopper had passed over, and an ATV team had run a perimeter search from shuttle stops out along a few of the trails, but in Matthew's estimation, it had not been an exhaustive search. Over the past few days, he and Dianne had taken the shuttle from one end of the park to the other, stopping one stop earlier each trip as they worked their way back. Today he was trekking south from the southern end of The Narrows, down the East Tim trail.

It was a long way on foot from where they had camped that night, and it wasn't likely Rick would have gotten so lost he went that way, but Matthew had to look somewhere and since all the probable places had been searched, he had to turn to the improbable.

Dianne wasn't with him, and though she was a good hiker, Matt had longer legs, so his pace was a little quicker on his own. He calculated the mileage again, estimated the time it would take him, the time left until dark, and began his day's hunt.

The trails were well-marked and well-traveled and for that reason,

Matthew stayed just off of them. If Rick had followed a trail, someone would have seen a sign of him by now. Matthew hiked within shouting distance of the East Rim trail, a six-mile journey along the eastern edge of the park. Matthew had been at it for hours and there wasn't a lot of sunlight left, but he was determined to make it at least the length of the trail before he quit for the day.

Matt sat on a copper-colored patch of flat stone and pulled out his trail guide and park map for the dozenth time that morning. He wasn't about to get lost himself, and he'd kept careful notes of where he'd been and how many times he'd been there. The park was vast and there was so much ground to cover it was overwhelming. Rick, one person without a map, without his phone, without provisions...

Matthew had to stop this train of thought. It would not do him or Rick any good.

He folded the map, put it and the trail guide in a backpack pocket, and stood. Then, startled, sat clumsily back down. There is nothing inherently unusual about ground squirrels, nor this one in particular, except it hadn't been there a moment ago. Squirrels are quick. They dart from rock to rock, plant to plant, seeming to appear out of nowhere. But this one was out in the open. This one wasn't between plants, between rocks, or up from a hole in the ground.

It was just there. It hadn't been, then it was.

The squirrel seemed startled too, as though it wasn't sure how it had gotten where it now found itself. It scurried a little one way, then another. Finding no shelter in any direction it was comfortable running, it sat stock still, apparently hoping stillness would render it invisible and thus out of danger.

Matthew watched it, transfixed. Staring wide-eyed at the confused rodent, Matt noticed something else unusual. He'd registered that there weren't any plants or rocks for the little rodent to hide behind just as the squirrel had, but he also noted it was the only patch in their immediate area where that was true.

It wasn't completely out of the ordinary to find a clean patch of land out here. It was rocky-desert terrain after all, but this little spot, a roundish not quite circular area about three feet across, was completely bare. There was a little dust, a few small pebbles, but nothing growing at all, no large stones, not even an insect scurrying around like the ants or beetles found everywhere else. There was nothing. Matt wouldn't have noticed it if it weren't for the squirrel, but now he could hardly see anything else.

He stood to have a look around, to see if there were other spots like this one. As soon as he did, the squirrel bolted and was gone.

Matt's jaw dropped. He stepped towards where the squirrel had been, searching in every direction from the rocks and undergrowth at the edge of the little bald spot and up the branches of the nearest shrubs. But there was no sign; not so much as a fluttering leaf. Matthew knew in his gut the little guy had not left the odd little patch of earth, but reason told him it could not have simply vanished. He stalked around the area, his eyes laser-focusing on every detail. The squirrel was gone.

Matthew took out his camera, the DSLR Dianne had bought him the previous Christmas, and took pictures of the bald spot and every tree, shrub, rock, and pebble in the immediate area. He turned on the flash and did it again, not taking any time to review the pictures as he snapped them, intent on getting every inch of the ground where he now stood.

He didn't know how long he'd stayed there, only that he'd burned a fair amount of daylight. He put the lens cap back on the camera and turned back the way he'd come.

6

It's Just Gone

"It vanished, Dianne! It appeared, then it vanished!"

"Matt, animals don't just disappear. Squirrels are fast. I'm sure you just missed it. Besides, you're tired. You're emotional. It's been an awful week and you're there by yourself."

It had been an excruciatingly long shuttle ride back to Springdale. He hadn't wanted to have this conversation on the shuttle where someone might overhear it. So, he'd waited until he was back in his hotel room. As soon as the door had shut behind him, he'd dialed Dianne.

"I know. I know what it sounds like, Dianne, but I am telling you it wasn't there, then it was, then it wasn't. And the surrounding ground, there was something odd. There was something different about it. Nothing was growing. There were no rocks, twigs, leaves. It wasn't even as sandy or dusty as the surrounding spots."

"And it was along the trail?" Dianne wasn't sure what the answer to that question was supposed to reveal, but there might be some clue in it.

"No. Not exactly. It was ten, maybe fifteen minutes' walk off the trail."

"Matthew, please be careful hiking off-trail. I don't-"

"I'm not going to go missing, honey. I promise. I had the GPS turned on on my phone the entire time. I dropped a pin in the spot so I can get back to it."

"Why do you need to go back? You said you got a lot of pictures of it.

Besides, you can't be out there forever. You need to spend your time looking for Rick, don't you?"

"That's just it, Dianne. That's what I'm saying."

"What? I don't understand. You think-"

"Yes! I just saw a damn squirrel appear and disappear out of thin air. If that's possible, maybe the same thing happened to Rick!"

Dianne was beginning to worry. Matt had always been a levelheaded guy, calm in the face of crisis. Even over the past week, he had had frantic moments but was calmer than most people would have been in the same situation. Now, he sounded like he was breaking. Dianne felt a weight in her stomach and wondered if she should have left him there alone.

"Matt, have you eaten today?"

"I had an egg wrap when I got back to Springdale after dropping you off at the airport and some gorp on the shuttle. I slept reasonably well last night too, before you ask. Dianne, sweetheart, I know it sounds like I am losing my mind. I know what it must sound like from your end, but you didn't see it. Have you ever known me to be irrational? Have I ever said anything totally nuts to you before?"

"Well, no, but the circumstances-"

"I know. I know. But... Rick could have just vanished!"

Dianne wasn't sure why this would be an exciting revelation. Even if it were not a complete fantasy, some kind of trauma-induced hallucination, the disappearance of their friend into thin air meant they would never find him. It wasn't as though Matt could follow him into... into the ether, into Neverland?

"Okay. Okay, Matt, suppose he did. Suppose Rick, like the squirrel, just vanished. What does that mean? If someone slipped through a crack in reality and vanished then-"

"But it appeared. That's just it, see? The squirrel vanished, yes, but before it vanished it appeared. Wherever it came from, it went back. It goes both ways."

"What does?"

Matt laughed, disconcertingly. "I don't know. It! The... doorway? The portal? If the squirrel can go both ways, reason would suggest Rick can too!"

"I don't know that reason has anything to do with it."

"Dianne. I'm going to order a pizza. I might even go out and find a six-pack. I need something to help bring me down a little. Then I'm going to go through all these pictures and see if there is anything I missed. I'll send them to you if I find anything."

"Okay. Matt, get some rest tonight. Call me before you got to sleep."

"It will be the middle of the night there by the time that happens."

"Well, text me at least. Let me know you're okay."

"I will. I love you."

"I love you too, sweetheart. Good night."

"Good night."

* * *

There was nothing unusual in any of the photos. There were dozens of them, and he'd flipped through them several times, inspecting each one closely, trying to find some anomaly, but there was nothing. He'd hoped to see a shimmer, a shadow, a ghostly glow, anything, but there was nothing in any of the pictures.

Matt pulled out his phone and again searched the internet for missing persons in the parks. Only this time, he added "vanish" to his search. When that brought him the same results he'd already read countless times, he read some of the more fringe blogs from the second and third pages of the search results; the ones that talked about the paranormal, aliens, psychic fields, anything that sounded like what he'd witnessed. He found not a trace of anything that wasn't completely nuts. It hadn't occurred to him that if he wrote a blog about the vanishing squirrel, people would think the same of him.

He found a Facebook group for people who had witnessed strange things in the parks. It was called "Paranormal Parks US." Matt joined it and posted the question, "Has anyone ever been in a national park and seen something appear or disappear?" He knew it was likely he'd get either no response or a flood of crackpots with ghost stories to tell, but it was worth a shot.

The pizza he'd had delivered wasn't bad, but it didn't hold up to what he was used to in New England. He hadn't gone out to get a drink but opted instead to hit a hotel vending machine for a Coke. Caffeine might not have been the first thing he needed, but it was that or bottled water, and Matthew could only tolerate drinking bottled water on a hike. Despite the caffeine and the adrenaline, he passed out atop the bedspread some time well into the night.

The next morning, he texted Dianne. "I'm sorry I forgot to message you last night. I fell asleep before I got a chance. All is well. Back to the trail today. Love you."

Before he set his phone back down, he noticed a notification of a private message from a person on Facebook he didn't know. He opened the app and read the message. "Stop looking." It was from Woodrow Wilson.

Though it wasn't likely to be from the actual, late former-president, the name, combined with the profile picture of a dead commander-in-chief, was a little unnerving. Matt clicked on the name to visit the sender's profile page. There wasn't one. He got an error message that told him that the page he had linked to did not exist. He refreshed the page. Same message. Opening the messenger app again, he tried copying the profile link into another browser window. Same result.

"Stop looking?" Matt thought. "What the hell?" He navigated to the post he'd made in the Paranormal Parks group the previous night. The post wasn't there either. In fact, there was a notification that someone had flagged it as inappropriate and it had been deleted.

"Maybe it was the ghost of Woodrow Wilson," he thought. He added another post to the page. "Who is Woodrow Wilson, besides a deceased, turn of the century US president?"

Then he called Dianne. She was in class and didn't answer. He left a message. "Okay, so I know I sounded crazy last night, but I have something maybe not as science fiction sounding but definitely as strange to tell you." That would get him a call back as soon as she got the message.

With no intention of telling them about the events of the past twelve hours or so, Matthew called his parents. They would want to hear he was okay. Mom would want to know when he was eating and sleeping and dad, if he took a turn on the call, would ask him when he was coming home and whether he would get fired for staying in Utah too long. The call went almost exactly like that. He considered his duty done, and it had been comforting to hear their voices if nothing else.

Then he called Grandma Rose. Her voice was the one he most wanted to hear. She was the one he could actually tell because even if she thought he'd lost his mind, she wouldn't say it. She'd encourage him to follow his gut. She'd tell him what his grandfather would have done, and that was all he needed. If his grandmother approved and his grandfather would have done the same, it was good enough for him.

"So, after I was through looking at all the pictures, I did some searching online to see if anyone else had experienced something similar. I found a lot of wild stuff; alien abductions and the paranormal, but nothing like what I saw with the squirrel. I found this Facebook group for people who've had weird park experiences. I figure I'm going to hear the same kinds of nonsense, but I posed the question anyway. Then I fell asleep. This morning, there's this message from someone using Woodrow Wilson as their profile name telling me to stop looking. I went to the guy's profile page, and it's not there! Grandma. This is getting crazy!"

"What do you think this person meant by 'stop looking?' You think he meant stop looking for your friend or stop looking into the disappearance phenomenon? I suppose it could be both, especially if they're related."

"I don't know. It's weird though, right? You think someone is just trying to spook me?"

"I don't know much about how Facebook works, but it seems like a lot of trouble to go through to spook someone. Besides, who would do that?"

"You're probably right. I don't suppose grandpa ever mentioned anything about disappearances, missing persons, squirrels popping out of thin air?"

Grandma chuckled. "No. He talked about the search and rescue you guys saw in the Green Mountains that time. He followed a news story for a while about a woman who went missing in New Hampshire while out hiking with her family. But I don't think there was anything else. I'd have remembered stories about vanishing squirrels."

"Yeah. You probably would."

"He kept a trail diary for a while, back before you two were hiking together. Sometimes he made little notes in his field guides. I could have a look if you think it would help. Maybe he saw something he never told me about."

"That would be nice if you have the time."

"What the hell else am I going to do?"

Matt and Rose shared a laugh. She asked, "So, are you going to stop looking like President Wilson told you?"

"No. He might have helped set up the national parks, but he isn't going to keep me from searching one."

"Atta boy. Love you, kiddo."

"Love you too, Grandma."

Matt knew there was almost no chance there was anything in his grandpa's trail diaries or field guides. He'd never looked at one, didn't know Grandpa Cliff had kept them, but he suspected they contained notes about what wildlife he'd seen, trail conditions, and weather. He'd surely have told Matt or Grandma Rose if he'd ever seen anything appear out of nowhere.

Matt thumbed the pocket watch that hung from his walking stick and wondered if grandpa kept any secrets for fear of sounding crazy, or perhaps out of fear of the ghost of Woodrow Wilson.

7

The Ghost of Woodrow Wilson

March first, 1872 saw the creation of Yellowstone as America's first national park. In August 1916, President Woodrow Wilson created the National Park Service as a bureau under The Department of the Interior. One hundred and two years later, President Wilson took to Facebook to send private messages to a research assistant from New Hampshire, warning him to stop looking for a missing friend in one of those parks. Matthew would have preferred encouraging words from the late John Muir, but that wasn't his kind of luck.

A message from a dead president with a defunct Facebook profile was one thing. Two messages from a dead president in under twenty-four hours was more than twice as strange. "Dangerous," was all it had said. The message increased his curiosity. It further confounded him who the sender might be and what his or her purpose was in sending the messages. It started his mind racing again, but the message itself left a lot to be desired.

Matthew thought it was safe to assume searching was what the message was telling him was dangerous, but how was it dangerous and why? Was it his physical searching in the park that put him in danger, or was it scouring the internet and looking for clues on Facebook groups?

The sender's first message could have been taken one of two ways; as a threat or a helpful warning. He was being chastised or someone was looking out for him. This second message cleared up the question. Someone was trying to protect him, but with no indication of what or who he was being protected from.

That morning, two items so occupied Matthew's mind he hadn't had time to mourn the disappearance of his friend. Rick went missing, and that was where the strangeness had begun, and it was the strangeness which riveted Matthew and had taken all his mental real estate. First, there was the patch of ground a short walk from the East Rim trail where he'd spotted the ground squirrel and watched its unlikely appearing and disappearing act. The other was the messages.

He kept coming back to his conversation with Dianne. His rational mind knew she was right. Squirrels can't just appear and disappear. But he knew what he'd seen. Sure, the little guy could have shot out from between some rocks and darted away into the thick of a desert shrub. That made sense. That's what squirrels do. But this one hadn't, and he couldn't help but assume Rick's disappearance could have happened the same way.

The Facebook group had been little help. His first post had been flagged and therefore no one had been able to comment on it and the second, though it remained up, had been fruitless. Members of the group had posted several comments in response to his "Who is Woodrow Wilson?" query. Some had commented with photos, some with illustrations, and several with links to online encyclopedia and biography websites. Comments asked why he wanted to know, or what the question had to do with the group in which he'd posted it, and a couple comedians turned his question existential, "Aren't we all Woodrow Wilson?" or, "Who are any of us, really?"

Useless. Then the second message had appeared, and just as the first, it couldn't be traced back to a live profile. Matt considered contacting Facebook for support but suspected it would be an exercise in frustration and futility.

The entire day turned that way. No more rodents appeared out of thin air. More hiking revealed that nowhere else along the trail, or within reasonable hiking distance of it, appeared to have the same bare quality as the place he'd sat the day before. He'd looked through the photos again. He'd talked briefly to Dianne. He scrolled a few more conspiracy websites. Nothing brought him any closer to Rick.

Matt ended the day a little earlier than usual, contemplating going home.

It was hard to bear the thought of leaving without his best friend, but he was beginning to accept that there was nothing more he could do in Utah.

8

Rick

"I walked away to take a leak, that's all," Rick kept thinking to himself. "I walked away, not a hundred yards to piss, and I walked right back to where I started."

At least he thought he had. He'd retraced his steps as best he could in the dark. It wasn't as though he was deep in the woods. There were canyons on either side of him, for crying out loud. He couldn't have wandered that far. He'd been away from the site for fifteen minutes or so before he swallowed his pride and started calling out to Matt and Dianne. They hadn't responded. He knew sound would travel well. It was deathly quiet, and his voice would bounce off the canyon walls. There was no way his friends wouldn't hear him. But they didn't, and it made him wring his hands.

Rick spent the night searching, increasingly concerned he'd gotten good and lost. He'd wandered into landscapes he knew he hadn't seen before. On their hike that morning, they hadn't ascended or descended as much as he was doing in the dark. At least, he didn't think they had. As well as he could, he retraced his steps every time his surroundings looked different from what he'd seen earlier.

In the wee hours of the morning, bleary-eyed and exhausted, he found his way to what had to be the same river they'd hiked the previous morning. The slightest hint of dawn broke. He sat on the ground in a clearing along the Virgin River and decided to wait from someone to find him. He had been gone long enough that not only would Matt and Dianne look for him, but search and rescue would out too.

Only they never came. Rick listened for voices and watched for a helicopter, but to no avail. He was alone in The Narrows. It looked vaguely familiar to him. He was sure they'd hiked this way. He could not possibly be that far from the campsites.

Even if he hadn't found their site, surely he would have come across another. But he hadn't. He didn't have his phone with him to dial 911, or any other number for that matter. He didn't think he'd need to bring his phone to take a leak in the desert, so he'd left it at the campsite. He probably wouldn't have had signal this deep in the canyon anyway.

After what felt like a couple of hours, and reluctant to sit in place any longer, Rick tried to find his way back to the trailhead. He'd find someone along the way he could ask for help, and if he didn't, he would at least find the road and hail a shuttle back to the visitor's center. He never came across a trail. There had been no trail markers. There had been no people.

The sun climbed higher over red rocks as Rick scanned the ground then the horizon with every step. Sweat broke out on his brow, and he knew if he didn't hunker down in a shady place to wait out the heat, he'd put himself in danger. The only other alternative was that he found rescue, or they found him. Sitting in place and waiting to be found was not Rick's style. He was desperate to get out of the park and contact Matt and Dianne.

Morning had given way to afternoon when he heard the sounds of passing cars. There hadn't been many, but enough he could point himself towards them. He'd been starting to think, like the trail markers and campsites, the road might have vanished as well. Given the direction the sun was traveling, Rick oriented himself in what he was nearly certain was south and made his way along the road, eager to spot the nearest shuttle stop.

"I have gotten myself so lost nothing looks right," he thought. "There has to be a stop along here somewhere."

He knew if he got to the visitor's center, he'd be able to make contact. The shuttle driver could probably radio in and let someone know he'd turned up and help him reach Matthew. He'd chewed through what had to be a mile and a half to two miles with no sign of a shuttle and no road signs advertising stops or pointing to the visitor's center. The heat was getting intense.

Rick slumped on a patch of ground at the side of the road and wiped the sweat from his face with the sleeve of his shirt. There was no shade, but he couldn't walk any further without taking a minute to catch his breath. Water would be critical soon.

He gave himself a few minutes, then slowly rose to his feet. As he did, a car approached. The driver pulled to a stop beside him.

"You need some help?" The driver was a young guy, maybe seventeen or eighteen years old, dressed in cargo shorts and a t-shirt.

"Yes. Please. My friends and I were camping last night, and I got separated from them. I've been lost all night."

"You were camping out here?"

"Yes. Down in The Narrows. We hiked from The Temple of something or other... I think they called it, into the canyon. We stayed overnight. I walked away from our campsite; nature's call, and never found my way back."

The kid cocked his head. "Sir, I don't know where any of that is. Far as I know, there aren't any campsites anywhere near here. I don't think it's even legal on this land. I can give you a ride to town though. Maybe you could go to the police station, and they could help you."

"Sure. Great. Thanks." Rick couldn't parse what the kid was saying about illegal camping. Perhaps he didn't know you could camp in The Narrows if you had a permit. Not everyone around here would know the names of trails and landmarks either. He decided not to sweat it and took the offered ride back to town.

The hotel and their rental car were in Springdale. He remembered that. They had driven past a bunch of shuttle stops with all kinds of interesting names as they made their way north to the edge of the park the day before, but he knew for certain they had gotten on the shuttle in Springdale. The problem was, when he asked the kid how long a drive it was to Springdale, the kid had no idea where that was either.

He said, "The nearest town is called Roosevelt, you know, after the president..."

"Roosevelt? Not Springdale?"

"Yeah. I've never heard of any Springdale. Roosevelt's the only place I know, and I've lived around here all my life. Maybe it's out towards Union."

Rick shook his head, not knowing what to make of what the kid was saying. Less than half a minute passed in silence, then the driver stared over at his passenger, slammed on the brakes, and said, "Holy shit! You're one of them!"

9

New Hampshire

It was good to see Dianne, Matthew thought. It was good to be back in his own house, in his own kitchen, using his own coffee pot. It was nice to be warm and sit on a comfortable couch, but it had been an awful feeling boarding the plane without Rick, departing Utah one person short, certain there had to be more he should have done.

"Honey, you did all you could. Search and rescue did all they could, and they will keep looking."

"It's a cold case now."

"I know it is, but that doesn't mean they won't keep looking. Did you ever talk to Martha about a reward? I'm sure that would rally fresh volunteers."

"I did. She was contacting contact Rick's firm to see if they could help. She's not in any better position to put up a bunch of money than we are."

"I'm sorry. I don't know what to say. I'm just sorry," Dianne said.

"Me too."

Matt hadn't told Dianne about the second Woodrow Wilson message over the phone. He decided to wait and do it face to face. "So, I told you about that Facebook message I had yesterday."

"The one from a dead president? Yes, I remember that. Did you hear from Millard Fillmore today? Garfield?"

"No, smartass. I heard from the same dead president."

"Seriously. You got another message?"

"I did. This one was a single, not terribly helpful, and slightly worrying word."

"Spit it out."

"It said 'Dangerous.'"

"What? That's it? Dangerous?"

"That's it."

"Someone is seriously messing with you, Matt. What websites were you visiting? What forums were you posting in?"

"I visited lots of places. I read a lot of blogs and the comments on some. I watched a couple YouTube videos. The only place I said anything was the post I put up in that Paranormal Parks group on Facebook."

"Did you tell the authorities or report it on Facebook?"

"And say what? After I posted a question about watching a squirrel vanish into thin air, I got a couple of messages from Woodrow Wilson and his profile seems to have been deleted."

"Okay. I see your point."

Matt ran his fingers through his hair and sighed.

Dianne said, "I wouldn't worry about it. I mean, it's weird. The whole thing is weird, but I'm sure there's nothing to it other than some dumbass yanking your chain."

Though he wasn't sure he agreed, Matthew replied, "I'm sure you're right. It's just not making any of this easier. You go to the vigil?"

"No. I couldn't make it. Between catching up on assignments and some work business that needed my attention, I couldn't get away, but I sent flowers to Martha from both of us."

"Like you would for a funeral?"

"I sent irises. They represent hope. Martha would know that. You know the kind of gardener she is."

"Okay. I guess that's good. I'm turning in early. Would you care to join me? I'd rather not go alone."

Dianne took Matthew's hand and led him to bed where, after taking off his clothes and getting comfortable, he immediately fell sleep. Dianne curled up against him, listening to him breathe and wondering how much of Matthew had come home and how much was still in Utah.

* * *

The first day back to work had been routine. Matthew had done everything he could to keep it that way. Consistency and predictability would be close companions if he wanted to keep his mind in New Hampshire, rooted in his daily life rather than trailside in Utah.

The professors he normally worked for had been understanding. For the most part, they sent their "best wishes" or prayers. There was even a condolence, though Matt wished there hadn't been. The academics had all been patient, knowing Matt would be out of town and knowing that it would take a couple days to get caught up and get his feet under him.

In the afternoon, Matt took his regular lunchtime walk to meet Dianne. They shared a veggie sub, sipped iced tea, and didn't talk about Rick, Utah, squirrels, US presidents, or anything that wasn't wholly grounded in the here and now. It took effort and Dianne had to remind Matt it wasn't denial or an attempt to bottle up or escape what they had gone through, but a break from it to re-center in normal for a while.

"What's new at work?" She'd asked.

"Nothing. Same old, same old. Dr. Alcorn is having me vet some research for an interesting paper he's writing on the role of New Hampshire in the Revolutionary War."

"I'm sure there are lots of those already. What makes his different?"

"I don't know yet. There are existing papers. I've read several today. What about you? What's new in the master's degree world?"

"Nothing. It's just work. Though, in other news, this morning the White House announced a budget proposal that seriously cuts funding to public lands. Speculation is it's another step closer to turning that land over to energy companies and real estate developers. I've been talking to a few of the other organizers on the east coast. I think we're going to have to mobilize on this one."

"Really? It's been a little while since you had to put feet on the ground."

"Don't worry," she smiled at him, "I've still got it."

"I know you do."

Dianne had been volunteering for pro-environment groups for as long as Matt had known her. Her passion for the matter was a force of nature. Shortly before beginning her master's degree courses, Dianne and a good friend she'd made on the protest circuit, Linda Thompson, had started their own non-profit "Earth Action." They were skilled at what they did. Dianne had developed a reputation as someone who could bring attention to important environmental issues and affect change. Though she always had some project she was working on, and they were all important to her, it had been several months, if not longer, since she'd had the gleam in her eye Matthew now spotted.

For him, the rest of the day had been like the rest of any other. He wasn't caught up by the end of it. It would take several more days to get there, but he wasn't drowning either. Dinner at home was quiet. Dianne picked a crime drama to watch, but it turned out to involve a missing person case, so Matthew took over the remote and turned to Netflix to look for a quiet nature documentary they hadn't seen. Before bed, he suggested they plan a trip to Waltham to visit his parents and check in on Martha. What he really wanted, what he needed to do, was see his grandmother.

10

Presidential Library

The second day back to work started as most mornings do; everything routine, everything exactly as expected. It was a few minutes before ten when that changed. Matt could always overhear the librarians at the front desk if he listened hard enough. They were normally just voices in the background, listened to but seldom registered. Sometimes, a conversation might pique his interest, or he'd overhear a familiar voice and tune in, but usually it was just ambient chatter.

Then it wasn't.

"Well, Matthew is a university research associate. Most of what he does is for the Ph.D.'s in residence, but he helps me out from time to time too. I think this is really up his alley."

"Very good. I should go find him then?" A man with a soft, warm voice replied.

"He just got back from a trip, so he's a little busy but I'm sure if you tell him you're working on a paper about the national parks he'll find the time. He's an outdoors kinda guy."

"Excellent. Thanks."

"He's just back that way. Can't miss his desk."

Matthew pretended not to have been listening. Facing his computer monitor, with an open file folder in front of him on his desk, he stared at anything but the man who approached. On any other day, he wouldn't have thought twice about helping a stranger find what he needed in the library. There was a satisfaction to be had connecting people with their research interests, but a stranger coming in looking for information on national parks on the heels of what he'd just been through stood the hairs up on the back of his neck.

"Pardon me," the man said.

Matthew ran his hands through his hair and said, "Just a moment, please. Sorry, I'll be right with you."

The man sat in the chair across from his desk and Matthew stole a glance out of the corner of his eye. The stranger was about his father's age; perhaps older or a little more weathered. He was dressed in a tan overcoat and was holding a gray, herringbone flat cap across his lap. He had on a pair of thick-rimmed bifocals through which peered intense brown eyes.

Unable to avoid it any longer, Matt lifted his face to the man and said, "Hi. How can I help you?"

"I'm looking for information on the US National Park Service, specifically its early history. I'm told you're the man to see."

"I can't claim to be an authority on the subject, but the parks are an area of interest for me, yes."

"And do you know much about their history?"

"Some," Matt said.

The stranger just looked at him as if waiting for him to say more.

Matt took a deep breath and uttered two words. "Woodrow Wilson?"

The man smiled, inclined his head slightly, and said, "People usually call me Roger."

"Is Roger your real name?"

The man smirked. "It might as well be. So, are you the man to help me with my research?"

"I might as well be." Matt fixed Roger with a cross expression. This was absurd, he thought, but he could do nothing more than play along. Dianne was right. This was probably some obnoxious prank in poor taste or a con, and the only way to get to the endgame was to play along. He asked, "Do you have a specific thesis you're working on? That's a good way to narrow the research."

"Well, I am looking into the reason the parks were formed."

Matthew fixed him with a sidelong stare. "Why? I guess I thought that was a simple answer, hardly worth a dissertation; protection and preservation."

"It seems simple, yes. And maybe it started out that way, but the parks have expanded a great deal over the years and I'm curious, particularly in the early days, what caused such rapid expansion."

"Okay…" Matt trailed off.

"Early history; turn of the century and on to 1970. Roosevelt to Nixon or thereabouts?"

"That's quite a scope; about a dozen presidents?"

"Yes. Those were big days for the parks, as I'm sure you know. A lot of land gathered up under the park system umbrella over those years. I'm curious about how the expansion happened. Why were those specific areas placed under protection and inclusion in the National Park Service? Why so many in the first part of the 20th century?"

"I'm sure I can help locate information like that. I won't be able to get to it right away, but-"

"There's no rush. Nothing is going to change between now and whenever you have time to do your reading."

"Oh, I can only *do* the research for professors here at the university. The best I can offer you is a list of texts and some suggestions on where to look for periodicals and published papers. I'm sure there are things you can find in the public record if you know where to look."

"I see. It may be useful to examine things that aren't public records. You know, I might mention that it isn't the politics of the thing I'm interested in necessarily, rather the politicians; well, the politicians and the others… power players."

Matthew thought about this statement for a minute. He sipped his now lukewarm coffee to get some moisture back in his throat and said, "Power players involved with the national parks?"

"Oh certainly. There are always power players, and they always have their private reasons. That's the order of things, you know. Well, I appreciate your help. Shall I leave you to it then?"

"Leave me to it? You aren't going to have a look at the resources I can point you to?"

"No. I think it's something you can handle when you have a few minutes. Like I said, no rush."

"How can I contact you after I've had a look?"

The man stood, donned his cap, adjusted his glasses, and said, "That wouldn't be a very good idea at all," and walked away.

* * *

"I should tell Dianne," Matt thought, then immediately replaced the thought with the reasons he shouldn't. He knew her opinion on the matter was this whole thing was some elaborate hoax. He wasn't sure what the purpose of said hoax would be or why someone would go to such lengths to pull it off, but he also couldn't explain it with anything better.

As much as hated keeping anything from Dianne, he decided to tell her he had some work to do and would be late coming home. She would assume he was catching up from his absence. If he did the work he intended to do, and it resulted in anything noteworthy, he would tell her about Roger then.

At the end of his shift, he let the librarians managing the front desk know he was off the clock but was going to stick around to work on some personal research. They didn't need to know this, but it was polite code for, "Just because I am still in the building doesn't mean I'm available to help."

The bread and butter of Matthew's job was collecting research, vetting it, and passing on synopses and notations to Ph.D.s working on papers. What he was doing that evening was much the same, except he wouldn't be passing the research on. He had no way of knowing if Woodrow Roger Wilson was coming back, when he was coming back if he returned, or what it was the man would want from him.

"So, the research is for me," Matt concluded. It wasn't as though this was a revelation. His conversation with Roger had clearly been about pointing Matt to things Roger already knew, but he needed to say it aloud to orient his mind. This was research he needed to absorb rather than sift and sort for someone else.

To focus his research, Matt tried to recall every detail of what the man had said. It wasn't difficult given the conversation was etched in his mind. The history of the parks, the reason for their creation and expansion, the power players involved; it all added up to something. How did it connect to the warning he had been given to "stop looking" or that his pursuit was "dangerous?" It made little sense. Matthew decided it might once he started digging.

* * *

The creation of the parks beginning with Yellowstone in 1872, the creation of the National Parks Service under Woodrow Wilson in 1916, and the developing mission of the department were all well documented. Matthew had read through what he'd gathered on those topics in under an hour. Much of it was familiar to him as a devoted and frequent visitor to lands managed by the parks department, and he knew where to look.

"Nothing unusual here," he thought, seeing no dangerous territory and absolutely no connection to missing persons.

Matt read about the lands that had been designated as national parks, conservation areas, and sanctuaries by Teddy Roosevelt, the parks turned over from the War Department or the Forestry Service to the National Park Service in 1933, and the historic preservation efforts undertaken by the Park Service beginning in the late 1930s. He researched to 1970 when congress passed an act affirming the authority and management structure of the Park Service.

All this research helped complete a picture of how the parks had gotten to where they were present day, but it didn't get him any closer to understanding why he'd been given this homework assignment. Was he meant to be finding something relevant? Was he meant to be on a wild goose chase? He had almost quit but chose to delve one layer deeper before retiring for the night, knowing that if he didn't, he'd be up all night wondering what he'd have found if he had.

"The players," Matthew thought. "Maybe I start from there and see if anyone mentions vanishing squirrels." He made a list of names he'd come across and ones he knew from his own experiences and reading. There was David Grimm, considered by many to be the father of the parks, John Matthews the first director of the Parks Service, George Carver who championed resource conservation, Teddy Roosevelt, Franklin Delano Roosevelt, and Woodrow Wilson.

In addition, there were respected congressmen from several states and across multiple generations who championed the expansion of the parks system, and notable scientists from a variety of disciplines who lobbied for park protection and management. There were even a few wealthy industrialists on the list; magnates who'd funded pro-parks campaigns or, in some cases, donated land. No names stood out. There were no obvious connections among them other than a passion for the parks.

He dug deeper into the political records, campaigns, and notable speeches of the biggest names on the list and came up with no more than he'd had when he started. His understanding of American politics may have deepened a little, but there was nothing in the public record that seemed to connect to connect with the sort of information Roger to want him to find.

Maybe the power players weren't the obvious ones; the presidents and the park's founders, Matthew considered. Maybe the influencers were behind the scenes, among the congressmen, scientists, and industrialists. Matthew focused on that section of the list and again there was almost nothing about them that stood out.

Almost.

Thomas Alan Baker was on record as having campaigned against a proposed budget measure in the late 1930s that would have cut funding for the parks. T.A. Baker was a physicist from Los Alamos known to have worked on the Manhattan Project and whose name also appeared on conspiracy sites referencing the Philadelphia Project in 1943. There was no reference in any biography Matthew skimmed of a personal connection between Baker and the parks, conservationism, environmentalism, or anything else that would have connected the dots. "Maybe he was just a fan of hiking or liked trees," Matthew thought.

Then he came across another name, Frederick Mason. "An astronaut?" Surely, he'd been recruited to speak to congress on a parks-related cause based on his celebrity. Celebrities do that more commonly than most people are aware of, but Mason hadn't done it publicly. In fact, Baker and Mason had only been obliquely referenced in public records regarding National Park Service related budget hearings.

Then there was a photograph that caught Matt's attention. It was an opening ceremony picture taken at Olympic National Park in 1938. Front and center was Franklin Delano Roosevelt. On his right was David Grimm with his long graying beard, wearing a neat suit and a smile. Flanking the president on the Left was Elijah Perry, governor of Washington state according to the caption. On either side of these three men were several dignitaries, local and state, and a few children who had probably won a trip to the opening ceremony with an essay. Matt jotted down every name he didn't recognize.

It was in the second row he saw three men who had, as far as he could understand, nothing to do with national parks, Olympic, or the state of Washington.

The photo caption named them as David Margo, secretary of defense, Aldo Humphrey, director of the Federal Bureau of Investigation, and Marco Bozer, physicist. They were faces that didn't belong together, much less in a photo from the opening ceremony of a national park. Matthew now had several lists of names. On those lists were circles, checkmarks, cross-outs, and asterisks that only Matt himself could have deciphered. He leaned back in his chair, unsure where to go next when he noticed the time.

"Shit!" He said to himself as he logged out of the computer, stuffed his notes in his backpack, and headed out to the bike rack to make his way home.

11

The Order

The Order was created, as far as modern historians are concerned, in the late 1860s during American reconstruction. It was a fraternal order for over a century, publicly admitting women during the civil rights movement of the 1960s, though some experts suggest there were secretly women members or even a parallel, women's only Order much earlier.

The Order's mission was, as any member would be happy to relate: "To gather together the thinking minds and concerned citizens of the United States of America to share discourse and foster ideas which strengthen and further the ideals and goals of this great nation and to work towards bringing such ideas into being."

Historians, editorial writers, and conspiracy theorists alike analyzed and parsed the vague language, each interpreting it to serve their own purpose or research. Members of The Order, or those publicly connected to it, defended the mission statement as being transparent and likened their organization to the salons of the French renaissance or the Royal Society of London.

There were no books written suggesting The Order performed arcane rituals. There had never been a documentary Matthew could find about The Order having connections to the Knights Templar, mobsters, foreign governments, aliens, or satanic cults. They appeared to be a club, albeit a somewhat exclusive club joined only by invitation. They had no website, no social media presence, and no public address or contact information. They weren't exactly a secret society, but they also weren't looking for attention or engaging with the public directly. The other thing Matthew had learned was The Order counted among their past members almost every name he'd circled on his list; the scientists, the industrialists, and the politicians.

The Order and the national parks were connected. "There are always power players. That's the order of things." Roger had said.

"He was trying to give me a shortcut, and I missed it!" Matthew thought. It was also possible he was supposed to recall Roger's statement only after he'd uncovered the apparent connection, to confirm he was on the right track.

"So, maybe Roger wanted me to see the connection to The Order, but all I see are members who championed the parks or showed up at a dedication ceremony. What the hell does that tell me?" He asked Dianne that evening, after he'd gotten home.

"I have no idea. I can't believe this freak has you so deep down the rabbit hole, honey. What's next? You can't spend all your time digging when you don't know what you're digging for or why." She topped off their coffee mugs.

"I can't walk away from it either. Dianne, you have to admit it's at least interesting, and it looks less like a hoax all the time. What I don't understand is the connection between the messages I got when I was in Utah, this research, and Rick's disappearance."

"I don't know if there is one. It still seems fishy to me," Dianne said.

"I understand that's your instinct, but I can't figure out what someone would gain by winding me up like this."

"You are wound up." She sighed. "So, what's next?"

"Well, I think the 'power players' Roger referred to might be the people in the photo plus Baker and Mason or it might be The Order as a collective power player. That seems to be the *who*. The *where* is the national parks, I think. I'm trying to look at this as a journalist. The *when*; Roger gave me the dates to look at. What, why, and how are the remaining questions as far as I can reason."

"And how are you going to answer them?"

"Read."

Dianne replied, "I had a hunch."

"You can help," Matt smiled at his girlfriend.

"Oh, can I?" She said, then smirked.

"Yes. You could take the names of some of these environmentalists, activists of their time, and see what you can learn about them. You'd know where to look better than I."

"That's your job."

"Yes, but they are in your field."

"And you have an entire sea of red herrings of your own to fish for."

Matthew looked over the rim of his coffee cup at her with an affected "I am not amused" expression and cracked a smile.

* * *

All the names Matt had jotted down were members of The Order. It had been easy to confirm. He'd read bio pages and Wikipedia entries on every one of them. Most of the bios mentioned their membership. Others, he'd verified with a few simple searches. Rather than being secret, membership seemed more like a badge of honor among the privileged and elite. It was exclusive and exclusivity conveyed status.

The difficulty was figuring out what The Order had to do with the national parks or missing persons cases like Rick's. It was possible, as Dianne suggested, membership in The Order and support of national parks was coincidental. Matthew thought Roger would not have sent him on the hunt and mentioned "the order of things," were that the case.

"Besides, a little overlap is a coincidence. This much is something else," Matthew had asserted.

During lunch the next day, Dianne having been tied up in a meeting with a professor over a complicated assignment, Matthew sat alone at the Brew House Cafe and sipped a medium caramel latte from a white ceramic mug while looking over his notes. It occurred to him he had thought little about Rick in the past twenty-four hours. He'd gotten entangled in the strangeness that followed his friend's disappearance to the point where he'd lost sight of where it started.

"Rick is still missing," he thought to himself, "And The Order doesn't get me any closer to understanding what happened. Roger hasn't given me any answers."

He was no longer feeling the leaden weight of sorrow in the pit of his stomach he'd carried around Zion, but instead a heat that started behind his ears and in his cheeks. And he could feel tension stiffening his jaw. His best friend had gone missing. The park's Investigative Services had "suspended" the case. There was a mysterious jackass giving him research homework, which hadn't helped. All he had to go on were some loosely connected dots from half a century ago. "I want some damn answers," he said to himself.

He switched focus from his written notes to the browser app on his phone and typed the words, "Current membership of The Order," into the text field, and hit "search."

12

Rick

"I've heard about people like you," the kid said, jaw agape and eyes wide. "I guess I always thought it was some kind of conspiracy nonsense, but you're really one of them?"

Rick fixed him with an incredulous look. "One of who?"

"The people who appear."

"The what?"

"The people who appear. Uh... so, like there are these stories from all over the United States, maybe around the world too but I haven't heard any, about these people who suddenly appear out of nowhere. They show up all lost and confused. Sometimes they're sick or injured or something, but they don't know what happened or what's going on. They just show up."

"And you think I'm one of these people?" Rick asked.

"You totally could be. I mean look, man, you were wandering canyon roads, claiming you've been camping somewhere it's illegal to camp. You're looking for a town you think you stayed in that doesn't exist. Your friends are nowhere to be found. Dude, you either suffered like some head trauma or you are totally one of the people who appear."

"I wasn't wandering the roads. I made my way to this road so I could get back to town."

"Which town?" the kid asked, smirking.

"Okay. Fine. Maybe I'm a little confused. I'm leaning towards head injury.

I got lost. Maybe I fell in the dark and hit my head and I don't remember it. People who just appear sounds a little too 'Unsolved Mysteries' to me. It's a little crazy."

"So is thinking the town we're driving into, a town you say you've spent one night in already, is called Springdale and that there's a hotel there."

The kid pointed to a road sign that said, "Entering Roosevelt."

* * *

"I'm losing my mind," Rick thought. This was not Springdale. There were no familiar shops, no restaurants, and no hotels. Where his hotel should have been, there was a Denny's.

"You mind dropping me off here?" Rick asked.

"Yeah. Sure. Are… uh… are you going to be okay? I've got to go to work, but I can hang out for a few minutes if you need to…"

Rick got out of the car and closed the door. Walking around to the driver's side he said., "No. I'm good. I just need to clear my head, I think. I'll manage."

"Nice to meet you," the kid said.

Rick shoved his right hand through the open window and said, "You too. I'm Rick, by the way."

"Daryl. And good luck."

"Thanks."

Rick walked into the Denny's and sat, ordering a cup of coffee, a stack of pancakes, and a side of bacon. He was more interested in cellular and Wi-Fi signals than in breakfast, but as soon as he'd smelled maple syrup, he realized how long it had been since he'd eaten. The waitress took his order and as soon as she'd walked away, he began fiddling with his phone. There still wasn't any cell service, but the sign in the window promised free Wi-Fi; password "grandslam." It took a minute for his phone to configure itself, but it reconnected him to the world.

Rick typed out a group message to his mother, Matty, Dianne, and his employer. It read: "It's me. I got lost last night. I think it was last night. I'm in Roosevelt. It's got to be near Springdale, but nothing looks familiar. I'm not sure how I got here. Someone call me." He hit "send."

Of the available explanations, Rick was still thinking head injury and considered whether a hospital might have been a better first stop than Denny's. But his head didn't hurt, he wasn't nauseated, and his vision was clear. If another answer didn't present itself over breakfast, he'd find a doctor.

He opened the browser app on his phone and typed, "people who appear." The quick return of hundreds of hits took him aback. He'd half expected the kid to be full of it, but skimming the page summaries it appeared this was an actual phenomenon or a widely held urban legend.

Rick read about an eight-year-old kid who had wandered out of the mountains in Tennessee, a man in fly-fishing gear who had turned up in Ohio, and a young woman who showed up in a town in California claiming she had been wandering in the Sierra Madres for a week. According to the article, there were no mountains named that in California. The one thing these other "sudden appearances" seemed to have in common, was there was no official record of the people who appeared. The names, addresses, and social security information they offered didn't match any government or law enforcement databases.

Rick was at a loss for what to do next, besides drink his coffee, eat his pancakes, and wait for someone to call him back. "Someone *will* call me back," he thought as he forked the last bite of syrup-drenched pancake in his mouth.

The waitress came back scowling, carrying the check he'd just paid, "Is this some kind of joke?" She asked.

"I'm sorry?"

"We don't accept whatever funny money this is." She tossed the few bills Rick had tucked into the folder a few minutes earlier on the table.

"What do you mean you don't accept this? You don't take cash?"

"Sure, we take cash, but not Monopoly money!"

Rick was speechless.

The waitress continued. "I was thinking maybe they were foreign bills, but they say 'United States of America' right on them. You make those yourself? Well, how about using some real money?"

Rick shook his head, reached back into his wallet, and produced a credit card, not sure where to begin unraveling the cash issue. "Here, just use this," he offered.

A few minutes later, she returned to the table with another Denny's employee, this one the only guy in the building wearing a tie. "Sir," he said, "I'm going to need you to come with me."

"What?!"

"Sir, you have tried to pay your bill with bogus tender twice. Dining in this establishment then skipping out on your bill is a crime. If you can't produce legal tender or a valid credit card, I will have to call the police."

"I gave her cash, including a generous tip. She wouldn't take it. And that credit card is completely paid off. There's no reason-"

"If that's how you'd like to handle this, sir, Roosevelt police will be here shortly."

"Oh crap," Rick thought and slumped back in his booth. With any luck, his phone would ring, or he'd get a message from Matt or Dianne who could help clear everything up before the local police arrived.

13

First Contact

The Order didn't publish a membership list, but tabloids and conspiracy theory websites were only too happy to compile their own. With nowhere better to begin, Matthew added a few names he'd found in those places to his growing list. The plan was simple. He would choose someone from his list, not a well-known politician or business mogul, but someone less high-profile and maybe more likely to respond to a message from a stranger. He would choose someone, them on Facebook or Twitter, and send them a private message. "I need to talk to someone within The Order." It would say. "I'm not a journalist. I'm just looking for a missing friend."

His plea might get a response and it might not, but if it did, he could use the opportunity to question someone within The Order about their connection to national parks. There couldn't be anything dangerous in that. As likely as not, whoever he reached, if he reached anyone, would have no idea what he was talking about.

He drafted a message and sent it to three people he'd chosen from his list; a television celebrity, a historian, and an equities trader. If he got no response from them after a day or two, he'd pick three more.

Meanwhile, he needed to continue his research. There were two fronts. First, he wanted to keep at the assignment Roger had given him. He no longer entertained the idea this was a hoax. It was now about finding out who Roger was, how he was involved, and why he was helping Matt, if that was in fact what he was doing. Second, was the missing; Rick foremost among them. Whatever answer he was going to find might be uncovered if the two lines of inquiry intersected.

Noticing time had gotten away from him, Matt downed the last few mouthfuls of now lukewarm latte, jogged out of the Brew House Cafe, and mounted his bike. The bicycle was part exercise, part economics, and part environmental, but it was also meditative. It took focus and caution to navigate even a bike-friendly town like Durham.

Focusing on a task like pedaling through the streets around campus or between campus and his home in Dover left his subconscious mind free to stretch while his conscious mind got a break from inner dialog and worry. Bicycling wasn't as good as hiking. It lacked the immersion in nature that wiped away the modern world a good trail afforded, but it was far better than driving or the public transportation of cities.

The September air in New Hampshire was crisp, especially rushing across his cheeks and knuckles as he biked to the library. Leaves had been kissed by color, but not fully transformed as they would be in another month. A light frost was showing in the ten-day forecast and that meant a little more bundling up for the bicycle commute, but Matt intended to travel under his own power until public transportation or riding with Dianne, depending on her class schedule, would become a necessity.

Back at work, Matthew checked in with Suzanne, the librarian at the front desk, to see if he'd had any messages or visitors, half expecting another drop-in visit from Roger. There had been no messages and no visitors. Matt moved on to check email and voice mail, his typical post-lunch routine. He added checking Facebook, which he normally didn't bother with at work, but there was never any telling when a dead president might be in touch.

All communications turning up clear, Matthew returned to his research. He was enjoying Dr. Alcorn's assignment. He had learned his fair share about early New Hampshire history during his time at the university, but he enjoyed immersing himself in the lesser-known corners. Vetting local history was not nearly as taxing as sorting research from professors in the applied sciences where the language was beyond his lexis and required keeping a dictionary tab open in his browser.

Much of Matthew's work involved searching journal databases to find papers that matched the key terms or the thesis provided by the professor he was assisting. Sometimes it was straightforward work and sometimes it took creative searching; coming up with his own parameters and filters when the obvious ones returned little or no useful results.

Occasionally, depending on the topic, the hunt took Matthew in to the library shelves to pull journals that had not yet been digitized. This was far more common with history and the humanities than it was in science and technology, the latter topics changing and evolving at a pace where the most relevant research was fresh enough to have been written digitally.

That afternoon, Matt was headed into the stacks. He'd printed the call numbers for a couple titles on the early colonial days of New Hampshire, a diary written by a Concord farmer and a historical narrative of mid-18th century New England colonies. Matthew knew the stacks well enough he knew where to go without even looking. Scanning the shelves, reading spines, and looking at call numbers, Matt found what he was looking for in a matter of minutes.

He also found a title that was clearly out of place. It was not his job to relocate misplaced books, but as a professional courtesy, he did so when he found them. "White Mountains National Forest: A guide to New Hampshire Beauty and Conservation," was stuffed between two history texts. Matthew slid it off the shelf and found a sticky note had been adhered to the front cover.

"You're going to get hurt," it read.

* * *

"This is going too far!" Dianne said. "Hoax or not, this is too much. You need to take it to the authorities."

"And say what? I don't even know if it was meant for me."

"Of course you do! A threat, Matt. That's a threat, and I can't believe you aren't taking it more seriously."

"Unless it's a warning."

"A warning of what?" Dianne asked. "From who? Woodrow Roger Wilson, who you have no reason to trust."

"I also have no reason to doubt him, Dianne. I don't understand it, but I have to follow it."

"He had to have put it there when he visited you the other day."

"But he didn't know what I was researching then. I never told him. If he'd left it the other day, wouldn't he have put it somewhere he knew I'd be looking?"

"So, what? He snuck in the library sometime in the last 24 hours and left a note instead of coming to you directly? How did he know where you'd be looking this afternoon? He knows too much about you!"

Matthew started to bite the nail on his index right finger, then thought better of it and ran his fingers through his hair. "I don't know. I don't... maybe he came in while I was at lunch or after I left work yesterday."

"It couldn't have been lunch today," Matt reasoned to himself. There was no reason for Roger to have come in today. All he'd done was the research he'd been instructed to do. Then it occurred to him he had gone outside those parameters. He'd tried to contact members of The Order. But that had been minutes before he got back to his desk. "Surely Roger could not have predicted Matt's research, written a note, and hidden it on a book in the library that quickly. Could he?" Matt asked himself.

"What?" Dianne asked. "What were you just thinking? There's something you aren't telling me, Matthew."

Matt took a deep breath through his nose, sighed, and looked at Dianne. "I don't think it's connected. It was too soon after to be connected. I'm sure of that."

Looking at the expression his circuitous explanation was drawing on Dianne's face, he refocused. "Clearly, at least clearly as far as I'm concerned, there is some kind of connection between The Order and the national parks. By itself, I guess that isn't so unusual. Clubs and fraternal orders take a special interest in issues all the time. Roger would not have put me on this path if that's all it was. There is no direct link between The Order and Rick's

66

disappearance. There's no obvious reason why it would be dangerous or why I was warned to stop looking."

Dianne folded her arms across her chest, her left foot tattooing the yellowing linoleum of their kitchen floor.

"The Order doesn't exactly publish a newsletter detailing the causes they've taken up, so I decided I needed to ask someone," Matthew continued

"Ask someone? In The Order? Ask them what?"

"Well, I haven't spoken to anyone yet, but I sent messages to a few social media profiles."

"And what did your messages say, Matthew? 'Hi. I'm Matthew. I'm a research assistant at UNH. My friend went missing in a national park. Then a guy calling himself Woodrow Wilson warned me off my search. Then he showed at my work and gave me a research assignment. That homework led back to you. Do you make people in national parks disappear? By the way, I saw a squirrel vanish once.'"

Matthew felt a tightness in his chest. He took a few deep, even breaths and reminded himself that Dianne was only worried about him, as sarcastic and possibly insulting as her question had been. "In so many words, yes. I left out the squirrel though, for now."

Dianne stood and straightened some dishes on the counter that didn't need straightening. Silence hung in the air like a two-day-old birthday balloon. "Honey," she said without turning around. "You have to stop. Rick isn't coming back. This Roger person is… I don't know what he is, but I know that he can't bring our friend back." She turned to face him. "And reaching out to some elite social club whose members support the parks where people go missing won't get you any closure. It will get you labeled as a nutcase."

Matt absently stirred his coffee for a silent moment before saying, "It isn't just about Rick anymore. Do you know how many people go missing in national parks? Do you know how many cold cases there are? No one knows why that is. On top of that, there is an organization or at least several members of a semi-secret organization who have a connection to the parks for no obvious reason. You're right. I can't get Rick back. I probably can't get any of them back, but don't their families deserve some answers? Don't they deserve some closure?"

Dianne walked around the counter and behind the chair Matthew occupied and put her arms around him. "I worry," she said.

"I know. I need you to trust me, though. I haven't lost my mind and I will watch my back, but I have to keep following this."

"I don't like these warnings or threats you're getting, Matthew. Have you at least thought about contacting the authorities?"

"I have. But I can't do that yet. If I give them a description of Roger and tell them he's been harassing me, they might scare him off. And so far, he's the only one who seems to have any idea what the hell is going on. I am going to describe him to Suzanne and the other librarians, so they can at least let me know if and when he's been around. Fair?"

"I'll support you here, Matt. You know I will because that's what we do, but on one condition."

"Which is?"

"If I think it's getting too... weird or dangerous. If it looks like you're tipping over the edge of something we don't understand, I get to call it quits and pull you back."

"Deal."

14

Earth Action

In the mid-two-thousand-teens, Dianne was the community organizer be-hind a successful campaign to stop industrial development in Massachusetts Bay. A firm with a questionable history had surveyed the area for the proposed development. The company who conducted the environmental impact study had conducted a study a few years earlier, which green-lit a project resulting in poisonous groundwater in several mid-western communities.

The campaign had put Dianne in the spotlight as far as organizing resistance against government policies which allowed for the destruction of natural resources or big business practices that resulted in damage to the environment was concerned. She was asked, from time to time, to provide a quote to the Boston Globe or a sound bite for her local NPR affiliate. She'd appeared on the five o'clock news when the Back-Bay project had gotten down.

It was this success that convinced her it was worthwhile to pursue her master's degree in environmental law. She wasn't interested in practicing law, but she wanted to speak the language. If she was going to be called on to make statements, to organize movements, to mobilize grassroots conscientious objectors, she wanted to be damn sure she knew what she was talking about.

That morning she'd left the house tightly wound. Matthew was not a conspiracy theorist. In all the years they had been together, he'd only ever scoffed at UFOs, Bigfoot, The Illuminati, etc. But now he was trying to contact an elite organization many believed, despite their transparent exterior, held more secrets than the Freemasons, to see if they could shed light on missing persons cases, including Rick's.

Dianne thumbed her phone, considering calling Matt's parents to plan an intervention, but she'd said she'd support him, and making that call would be a betrayal. She could call Grandma Rose. If she were going to call anyone, it would be the person who knew Matthew best. Rose loved him dearly, and she would offer guidance Matt's parents might not. For the time being, she would be patient and keep a close eye on how things progressed.

Dianne unlocked the door to the Earth Action office, a small storefront, recently vacated, the organization rented for use as an office. It wasn't a nice place. It wasn't up to date, and it needed more than a fresh coat of paint, but it was theirs and it was what donations and sponsorships could afford. She sat at her desk and powered up the computer.

Linda burst through the door, "Guess what?" she said, waving both hands in the air. Linda was the other half of the allegedly paid staff of Earth Action. She was invaluable; dedicated to the cause, determined they would succeed at whatever they were doing, while simultaneously espousing defeat and nihilism.

"Oh! I brought donuts. I wasn't going to, but then I was like 'screw it' I totally am. So, here's a donut, bitch. Guess what?"

"Good morning, Linda. Thanks for the donut. What?"

"So, we got an email. Well, actually you got it and I read it so it's ours now. Anyway, you got an email from a congressman."

"Looking for money? Votes?"

"No! Don't poop my party. No, this congressman, who emailed from a personal email address, not his official state rep one; yeah I noticed that right away-"

"Hang on. How do you know it was really a congressman then?"

"You want me to take your donut away? I'll do it."

"I'm sorry. Go on."

"Damn right. So, president ass-hat sent his budget proposal to congress yesterday, and it has some garbage in it about opening federal lands to fracking and mining."

"I'd heard about that. I've actually been brainstorming what we can do about it."

"Good. Well, this congressman dude, he wants everyone to know how bad the budget would be. He wants to talk to you, well actually us now, sucker, about mounting a campaign for public awareness."

"Is he going to speak out on the floor? Are there hearings about it?"

"I have no idea. Probably. The email doesn't say all that. Even if it did, I probably wouldn't have read that far. Dude! We have a congressman who wants our help."

"He could want us to be the fall guy so if the budget passes he won't have egg on his face."

"You suck at excited, Dianne. Do you know that? I'm going to need you to work on it. I'll be at my desk, being excited, and eating my happy-donut while you sit there and eat your sad, skeptical one."

"Thanks, Linda. That's great news. I'll read the email right away."

* * *

The email had been no more and no less than Linda said it was. It was from Dan Sperling (D), Colorado. There weren't any details regarding what congressman Sperling wanted them to do, but there was an invitation to reply to the email if she was interested in discussing it further. Naturally, she was.

Congressman Sperling,

Thank you for contacting Earth Action. We are deeply concerned over the president's proposed funding cuts for federal lands, particularly the national parks, preserves, and forests. Opening this land for private use and ultimately allowing energy companies to develop it is a tragedy with far-reaching environmental impact. I would very much like to speak with you about how we can aid your fight in stopping this.

Respectfully,
Dianne Chambers

She hit send and let out the breath she didn't know she'd been holding. If this was what it appeared to be, it would be a genuine opportunity to make a difference. It was a national issue and that meant they could get supporters on board from all over the country. The more people they could rally, the more attention the cause would get, and the more they could do to fight.

"Linda, I replied to that email. I'll let you know when the congressman responds."

"Rock on. How was the donut?"

"Pretty happy actually. Thanks."

15

Networks

"It was from Dan Sperling, from Colorado. He's not a major name in the news, but we know who he is. He cosponsored a clean energy bill that passed in the house last year. That put him in the public eye, at least as far as environmental activism is concerned."

"That's great, honey. And you wrote him back?"

"Yes, first thing this morning. I haven't gotten a reply yet, but I'm sure I will. What about you? How was the day? Anything out of the ordinary?"

"Not exactly. I mean yes, but not a dead president, disappearing squirrel, anonymous sticky notes out of the ordinary. It must have been the day for big contacts though."

Dianne took a bite of her veggie wrap and waited. When Matt saw she was chewing through her pita, he went on. "I heard back from Kendra Riggle."

"Who?"

"Sorry. She goes by Danielle Lovejoy."

"The actress? I didn't know she was one of the people you contacted."

"Yeah, one of the sites I looked at the other day said she was a member."

"And?"

"And, we can talk about it later. I want to hear more about the congressman. Any idea what he wants you to do? Any thoughts on how you can help?"

"He didn't give any specifics. It could be anything from working together on a media campaign to organizing a resistance group, to him backing us on our campaign until the budget passes, then distancing himself from it, so we look like the radicals instead of him. It wouldn't be the first time we were in that position. What did Ms. Lovejoy say? I haven't seen her in anything for a few years."

"Apparently she's been on Broadway and working on some smaller, independent projects."

"She tell you that?"

"No. The internet did."

"So, what did *she* tell you?"

Matthew ran his fingers through his hair. "Not much, actually. She asked me, or maybe it wasn't even her, but a publicity agent or PR person, why I thought The Order would have anything to do with a missing person."

"I told her Rick went missing in a National Park and when I looked into disappearances in the national parks, I noticed over the years several prominent people connected to The Order had been involved with the parks."

"Did she respond to that?"

"Yes, but in a way I think it was probably a brush off. She told me it was news to her The Order had anything to do with the parks. She said she wasn't surprised, said they get involved in a lot of things, including some conservation and environmental issues, but she didn't know anything specific, said it wasn't clear how that connected to missing people. It took a minute for me to respond. I don't know how or even if it connects. But I didn't want to say that. I wanted to keep the connection open. So, I told her I thought with The Order's connections and resources they could help me find Rick."

"Any response to that?"

"No. Not yet, anyway."

"Do you think you'll hear anything back?"

"I… I don't know." Matt finished his BLT and crumbled up the paper its paper wrapper. He gathered Dianne's and took it and both their to-go cups to the recycling bin a few paces down the path.

"Well, I guess this afternoon will be all about waiting to hear."

"It looks that way. Have a good rest of your day. Good luck in class."

"Good luck at the library."

"I love you."

"I love you too."

* * *

"Anyone in to see me, Suzanne?"

"Nope."

"What about that guy I mentioned to you? Seen him today?"

"Nope. Everything okay?" she asked.

"Yeah. As I said, he's a little strange. I did some research for him the other day and I'm eager to go over it with him, but I think he slipped in and out while I was at lunch yesterday."

"Got it."

"Have a pleasant afternoon."

"You too, Matthew."

Matt walked to his desk and sat. He laid his messenger bag under his desk, leaning against one side like he usually did before he noticed it. His desk was a mess. It wasn't slightly disorderly or uncharacteristically disheveled. It was a disaster.

The folders he had laid in neat stacks to the right of his keyboard were spread across the desk, their contents spilled out in random heaps. The sticky notes and the notepad he kept near his phone for messages and reminders were altogether missing. The top desk drawer was ajar, having clearly been rifled through since the orderly arrangement of pens, pencils, and highlighters were not the way he liked them. His keyboard and mouse had been moved. Matt was certain his filing cabinet had been searched too, given that the top drawer wasn't completely closed. He knew if he opened it he would see folders askew and uneven spacing between the hanging partitions.

"There are two possibilities," Matt thought. "One of the professors was looking for some research I've done and was in a hurry." It wasn't impossible, Matt concluded. But everyone had his cell phone number and if he'd have gotten a call before someone went rifling through his desk. The other possibility was Roger, or someone he was associated with was looking to see what he'd learned.

"Roger?" He asked himself. It felt unlikely, but who else could it have been? Then it occurred to him, rather than Woodrow Roger Wilson, it could have been whoever Roger had been warning him about. Mat let out an exasperated breath.

He sat and reordered his desk. It took a few minutes before it was satisfactorily arranged. Deciding further organizing could wait until he'd settled down more, he tapped a key on his keyboard to wake his computer. The login screen appeared and Mat entered his credentials.

The desktop displayed on his screen was all wrong. Icons were missing. His recycling bin was empty. Opening the file explorer, he discovered the few personal folders he kept were gone. He could feel his heart rate climbing. His browser history was empty. He was logged into his email, though he knew he'd signed out before lunch.

Matthew picked up the phone on his desk and dialed the IT department. One of the grad student employees who worked tech support answered the phone.

Matthew said, "Hi. This is Matthew Conrad. I'm a research assistant working out of the main library. I just came back from lunch and… something is wrong with my workstation."

"What's wrong?" The IT guy asked.

"Everything on my desktop is gone. Some of my folders are missing. My browser history has been cleared."

"When did you last login to this account?"

"Just before lunch; about an hour ago."

"Okay. Let me look. What did you say your name was?"

"Matthew Conrad."

"And what login were you using?"

Matthew spelled out, "MConrad4793."

A pause. The tapping of keys. Another silence, then "You say you logged in before lunch? How long ago was that?"

"Thirty-five, maybe forty minutes."

"I have a login from thirteen minutes ago."

"I was in the quad eating lunch with my girlfriend thirteen minutes ago."

"Someone logged in as you. You're going to want to reset your password. You'll want to make sure it's a strong one. There are some suggestions on how to do that on the university IT page."

Matthew asked, "What about my missing stuff? Can it be retrieved?"

"Not out of the realm of possibility, but honestly man, it's not likely. I'll see what I can do and get back to you. Anything else?"

"No."

"I'll send you the link to change your password."

"Thank you," Matthew replied.

The support guy said, "Take it easy," and ended the call.

Without bothering to review the suggestions for a strong password, Matthew followed the link he'd received and came up with a twelve character, alphanumeric login he knew no one else would work out. Though, he had thought no one would work out the last one.

16

Close to Home

Grandma Rose sat in the green armchair in the corner of the spare room in her son and daughter-in-law's house in Waltham, Massachusetts. The armchair had been one of the few pieces of her own furniture she'd brought with her when her son cornered her into moving in with them. The chair was worn, approaching threadbare, sagged in the middle of the seat, and had cat scratch marks on three of the four legs, but it smelled like Cliff. It had been his chair. It was the chair he watched television from, the chair he read books in, and best of all the chair he'd told her stories from.

Her grandson Matthew took beautiful photographs when he went out into the wilderness. Usually printed in black and white, but sometimes in color, they were a thing of beauty. Rose had one above her dresser. She had no use for a mirror, figuring that she already knew what she looked like.

Cliff didn't take pictures. He told stories. He painted the same pictures Matt's photographs did, but Cliff did it with words. He could describe every kind of tree, fern, grass, and flower. He could paint the colors on every birds' feathers and the antlers on every deer. Rose adored listening to him. The old chair, it's worn patches, it's caved-in cushion, and its smell made her feel like Cliff wasn't so far away. Matthew made her feel that way too.

The two of them had been such close friends, Cliff and Matthew. Matt was so much like his grandfather sometimes talking to him made her feel like she was talking with her late husband. Rose had known the three of them would be close from the moment Matthew was born. Their conversations were easy. They skipped small talk and didn't gossip. It was just two people talking. They listened to each other. They confided in each other.

Grandma Rose pulled the smoothly worn lever on the right-hand side of the chair to bring the footrest up, planning a little nap when her cell phone rang. Most of the time she ignored it, but this was Matthew's ringtone. She'd asked him the last time they saw one another to set her up with a special ringtone so she'd know it was him. A nap could wait. Matthew needed her.

"Hi, grandma."

"Hi, honey. Somehow, I knew in my bones I would hear from you."

"Your bones are usually right. How are you?"

"Oh, I'm gray and wrinkled and closer to dead than alive, but I'm smiling." Matt chuckled.

"How about you, kiddo? How are you holding up?"

"Well... Okay, I suppose."

"Spit it out," Grandma Rose interrupted.

"What-"

"Spit it out."

Matt chuckled again, but this time it sounded to Rose like relief.

"Okay. Since Rick disappeared, about the time Dianne left Utah and came home, there's been some weird stuff going on?"

"What kind of weird stuff? Weirder than the squirrels? Is this why you asked me about grandpa keeping a journal?"

"It has something to do with that, yes. Did you have a chance to look for them?"

Rose replied, "I came across a couple, yes. I thumbed through them, but I didn't see anything out of the ordinary. What kind of weird, Matthew?"

"Weird like... hard to explain. It's... I'd really like to come down and see you, talk face to face. I miss seeing you anyway. It's just-"

"You know your mother and father can't handle 'weird?' You don't want mom making a fuss over how you're doing or asking you about Dianne? You don't want your dad to ask you about available promotions at work?"

"Something like that, yeah."

"Come down anyway. I'll come up with some kind of reason I need to get out of the house. I'll have your dad bring me to the senior center or something, then I'll get an Uber."

"You'll get an Uber?"

"Sure. Why not? Uber has something against old ladies?"

"Not at all." Rose could hear Matt smiling. She considered her job partly done already.

"You really are the best, grandma. I'll plan on tomorrow unless you can't get dad to take you, then we'll plan it for another time."

"Tomorrow is good. If your father won't take me, I'll Uber right from here, and he and your mother can both look at me like I'm nuts."

"Sounds good. I love you."

"I love you too. Try to stay out of anything too weird until tomorrow."

"You got it."

Rose hung up the phone and leaned back in the old green chair. She drifted off to sleep, smiling.

17

Rick

The police arrived. At first, they questioned Rick about trying to get out of paying his bill. When he explained he'd tried to pay twice and presented both the cash and his credit card, one of the officers escorted him outside while the other remained to finish up with the restaurant manager.

Having nothing to lose, Rick explained to the officer he didn't know where he was, didn't know exactly how he'd gotten there, and did not understand why his card declined or what the problem had been with his cash. The officer shook his head and examined the bills he'd taken from Rick.

He was pushed into the backseat of the police cruiser, having received no reply from the officer. When the second policeman left Denny's, he was on his radio, a bulky thing that looked to Rick like an old walkie-talkie or a satellite phone he'd seen in movies. The two officers chatted a moment, shared another look at the cash, and were back on the radio before they got in the car.

"Is this really necessary?" Rick asked. "All this over a payment snafu at Denny's? Am I under arrest? I haven't been read my rights."

Rather than answer his questions, the officer in the passenger seat, the one who had been on his radio asked, "Who is the president of the United States? What year is it?" Where and when were you born? What brings you here?"

Rick answered the questions in order but was certain from the officer's creased bow his answers were not satisfactory. The officer made notes in a small spiral pad he pulled from his pocket. They drove on in silence.

"I don't understand what's happening. Can one of you please tell me what's going on? I think I may have hit my head. None of this makes sense."

The officer in the passenger seat glanced at Rick in the rearview mirror but remained silent.

Upon entering the station, the two officers parked Rick on a cold metal bench along a wall in the corridor and told him to wait. After a discussion between the two officers and desk sergeant, he found himself alone in a cell the size of a gas station bathroom.

An hour passed. Then another. A plain-clothed officer visited sometime into the third. This officer carried a notepad and Rick's cash and credit card. He asked Rick the same questions the two officers who'd brought him to the station had. He answered as well as he could but had given up trying to convince them he was lost. The man walked back out the door he'd entered through and left Rick calling, "Please tell me what's going on!" which turned to, "You can't keep me here like this!" but no one responded.

Then the van came.

He couldn't see it from the cell, but it arrived just the same; followed by a pair of black Suburbans with tinted windows. Out of the van emerged two men in head-to-toe white jumpsuits with gasmask-like helmets. They carried between them a heavy-looking, footlocker-sized case full of gear. The gear was unpacked, doors, windows, and air conditioning vents were sealed over with plastic. Then two men in black suits and sporting earpieces stepped out of one of the Suburbans. They ushered the police station's officers into a small conference room and told them to wait.

Once everyone had been corralled and sequestered, with no small amount of arguing from the station chief, one of the men came through the door that prevented Rick from seeing any of what had just happened.

"Mr. Minor, is it?" the man asked.

"Yes. What the hell is going on here?"

"It seems we have some confusion, Mr. Minor." The man spoke in a calm, even tone.

"Confusion?" Rick was as impatient as the stranger was relaxed. "I've been arrested and left to rot for trying to pay for breakfast. I have no idea-"

He was interrupted. "Yes. The bills you offered the waitress, the ones the officers took off you, where did you get them?"

"Get them? I don't know; probably from an ATM. They might have been change from something I bought at the airport."

"I see. Which airport would that have been?"

"Boston. Logan. What difference does that make?"

The man said. "Mr. Minor, I need you to recount for me the events of the past forty-eight hours as best you can. Don't leave out any details."

"I've been through-"

"Indulge me, please."

Rick repeated everything he'd told the other officers. He started from The Narrows where and walked the man painstakingly through everything he'd seen, done, and heard until his arrest. The man didn't take any notes. He just listened, nodding from time to time.

"Rick; can I call you Rick? We'll need to talk about this further, but this isn't the place. I'm sorry you've had to sit here waiting all this time. We will get it straightened out, and we'll both get some answers."

"Am I under arrest?"

"No. A couple of my colleagues will be in shortly. There are one or two things we need to take care of, and we can depart."

"Depart where?"

The man didn't answer his question. He said, "Thank you for cooperating," and walked out the door. He was replaced by two men in white jumpsuits carrying a hard plastic trunk.

Rick backed up in his cell, hands thrust out in front of him. "What the-"

"Please remain calm, sir," a muffled voice behind a plastic mask said. "This is only a precaution. We are here for your safety and the safety of the men and women in this building."

"Precaution against what?" Rick shouted.

"Please step to the back of the cell and raise your hands above your head."

* * *

Rick was thoroughly sprayed with a dry foam from what looked like a yellow fire extinguisher. He sputtered and coughed, tried to protest, but it was clear this was happening with or without his cooperation. He threatened them when they approached. He tried to shove one of them out of the way, but they were deft on their feet and clearly trained to overcome his resistance. They weren't rough with him, but they would get their job done.

One of the men ran a wand of ultraviolet light over him while the other shined a penlight in his eyes, ears, nose, and down his throat. Blood was drawn. Hair was clipped from the top of his head. Though he'd argued and fought, the jumpsuit-clad men gathered their equipment, thanked him for his cooperation, and left him locked in his cell.

Two police officers came in a half-hour later and unlocked the door. They escorted him out of the back of the building and lifted into an unmarked, windowless panel van. The interior had opposing benches, parallel with the sides. Rick sat in the middle against one wall. The two men in jumpsuits, now face-shieldless, climbed in and sat across from him. Finally, the man in the suit who had questioned him stepped in and closed the door. Rick heard the front doors open and close, the engine start, and the thunk of the locks engaging.

"I know this has been unpleasant for you, and I am sorry about that," said the suit-clad man.

"Those pancakes were definitely not worth all this," Rick said.

The man chuckled. "I told you I'd get you some answers, and I will. First, I have a couple more questions for you."

"Of course you do."

"When you were lost, or rather before you realized you were lost, did you notice anything unusual in the park?"

"'Unusual like what?"

"You say you walked a short distance to relieve yourself and when you turned around, it seemed you had lost your way. Before you turned around, or perhaps while you were hiking earlier that day, did you see anything that felt out of place?"

"I felt a little out of place, but no I don't think anything like you're getting at. What *are* you getting at?"

"I see." There was a buzz, and the man fished what appeared to be an oversized smartphone or small tablet from his pocket. He thumbed through a couple of screens, nodded a few times, closed his eyes, sighed, then opened his eyes again, and put away his phone.

"What was that?" Rick asked.

The man said, "A bit of information about you, Mr. Minor."

"What kind of information?"

"It seems you don't exist." He said flatly.

"I beg your pardon."

"Rick, I'm afraid there is no record of you. Based on the information you have given us, you don't exist. The files I just received confirm it. A few of the minor details of your background line up, but not enough to verify your identity. You aren't in any government database. Thus, we are operating under the assumption that you don't exist. And if you don't exist, the question is, how are you here?"

Rick stared. There wasn't an answer to what the man was saying. He wondered if he was dreaming but knew in his gut he was not. "I…" he started, but the man in the suit cut him off.

"I think I can answer that question, at least in part, but not here. We've nearly reached our destination. When we arrive, you will be escorted to a single occupancy dormitory. There will be a change of clothes and some snacks and beverages will be in a mini-fridge in the room. There is no television, radio, or wireless communication available in the room. Please, try to relax until I or a fellow agent come to get you. You are in no danger as long as you present no danger. We will answer as much as we can. We appreciate your cooperation."

18

The Usual

The expression on her son's face was priceless as she strolled down the driveway to get in the sedan that had pulled up. She'd looked at her phone, looked at the face of the driver, and the license plate on his car, then up at her son who looked for all the world like he'd seen a spacecraft abduct his elderly mother.

Rose waved, smiled, and shouted, "I won't be long. I'm going to visit the girls," and hopped in the back of the car.

Sitting in a booth at a diner with her grandson a few minutes later, she said, "Oh, Matthew, you should have seen it. I'd have paid double the fare just to see that face."

"And you didn't tell him where you were going?"

"Nope. I said I was going to see the girls. He doesn't know who they are, or if there are any 'girls.' He just knew he couldn't argue with me because I was already gone."

Matt smiled and shook his head. "Grandma, you're a trip."

"I know. It's one of the reasons you love me."

"It is indeed."

Matt tucked another syrup-drenched forkful of pancakes into his mouth and sipped his coffee. Grandma Rose cut into the steak portion of the steak and eggs she'd ordered. "So, kiddo, tell me what's going on. You sounded shaken when you called. You okay? What's this weirdness you were getting at?"

Matthew took grandma back to the disappearing squirrel, walked her through the messages from Woodrow Wilson, the visit from Roger, the research, the sticky note in the book, and the private messages he'd sent members of The Order. He tried to recall every detail and present everything in precisely the right order. If grandma could help, he needed her to have all the information he had.

"Hmm," she said and wiped her lips with her napkin. She had said little as he was telling the story. She asked him to clarify one or two things or to repeat some detail, but otherwise, she'd just listened, her eyes fixed intently on him, her brow creased in concentration. "What does Dianne think of all this?"

"At first she thought it was all a hoax, though neither one of us could explain why someone would pull it or what the endgame was. Now, I'm not sure. She thinks I've gone too far. She thinks I'm cracking up, becoming a conspiracy nut, chasing ghosts. I don't know. My guess is it won't be long before she hands me the number for a grief counselor so I can 'process my loss of Rick in a healthy way.'"

"I can understand where she's coming from, Matthew. If it wasn't happening to you, but someone told you about all this, wouldn't you think they were a couple pancakes short of a stack?"

"Is that what you think?"

"Not at all. Listen. I've been around long enough to know the truth is often stranger than fiction as they say. I also know you're a levelheaded kid. So, I tend to think whatever this is, it's not the creation of some part of your mind that misses your friend and needs an explanation."

"So, what is it?"

"That is the question. Do you think this Order is behind the disappearances?"

"Behind them? My gut tells me no, but it tells me they know something about it."

"Okay. Go with your gut. What could they know?"

Matt stirred the syrup around his plate with the last bite of pancake. "Well…

they seem to be connected to the parks in some way."

Grandma interrupted him. "You've jumped a step."

"What?"

"Don't make assumptions. You have any evidence The Order is involved with the national parks?"

"Well-"

"You have photos of people at a ceremony, mentions in the records of people who happen to be members of The Order."

"I think I see what you're getting at. I have connections between people and the parks, and people and The Order, but not directly between the two."

"Right. Continue."

"So, there are people with connections to The Order who also have connections to the parks. Some of them are scientists, some politicians, some business moguls…"

"And?"

"And I don't know what else I have," Matthew replied.

"You have this Roger fellow who is trying to show you a connection."

"I don't know if I have Roger or if he has me."

"There's one clue I think you're missing. You said there are a lot of unsolved missing persons cases on federal lands, right?"

"Yes. Hundreds, thousands maybe."

"Are any of those cases connected to the parks these Order people?"

"I don't know."

"Listen, kiddo, I don't know what the hell is going on. I don't know if you ever will either. What I know is you won't give up. Something has gotten into you, and it's not just about finding Rick. You've picked up a scent and the bloodhound in you isn't going to let it go. You're like your grandfather in that way. You aren't crazy. That I'm sure of. Well, you're no crazier than any of the rest of us. My advice? Keep asking questions, but dig deep instead of wide. Pick a handful of these missing persons cases and investigate them yourself. Find the connections."

That was exactly the kind of thing Matthew had gone to see his grandmother to hear. First, that he wasn't crazy and someone had his back no matter what, and second, a fresh perspective.

While they sipped coffee and waited for the check, they shared stories; old stories about grandpa, about when Matt was a little kid, about holidays at grandma's house. And for a little while, Matt's life felt kind of normal. He had waited until his grandmother was in the back seat of her rideshare before he got in his own car and pulled away.

* * *

"Good afternoon, ma'am," the driver said. His ID and Uber profile showed his name was Malcolm.

"Good afternoon, Malcolm."

"I noticed you in the diner. Visiting with your grandson?"

"Yes. He's a sweet kid. He lives in New Hampshire."

"Just down for a visit?"

"Yes."

"That's nice. Now, ma'am," Malcolm said. "I'm going to need you to tell me everything you and your grandson talked about."

Rose wanted to interpret Malcolm's statement as a socially awkward way of continuing the small talk. "So, what did you two talk about on your visit?" or something like that. Then, she heard the click-thunk of the door locks and his question took a different tone.

"I don't think that's any of your business, is it? Stop the car. Let me out and I won't call the police. I have your information on my Uber app, including the make, model, and plate number of this car."

"Very resourceful, ma'am but you'll have to take my word it won't do you any good. I will be more than happy to take you home, collect payment for the ride, and depart as friends, but I am going to need you to tell me everything I want to know before that can happen."

Malcolm's calm, congenial manner was disarming. He had probably spent a long time honing it that way because beneath the polite smile was a make-no-mistake layer of cold steel.

"I'm not sure what you think I have to tell you."

Malcolm smiled back at her through the rearview mirror. "Now Rose, may I call you rose? We both know you weren't talking about the weather or the Red Sox potential for a solid October, so let's not insult each other's intelligence." Malcolm turned left at the first stoplight, where he should have turned right.

"This isn't the right way," Rose said.

"That's true. I'm afraid I'll have to make a few more wrong turns if you don't open up a little."

"What if I decide I'm not going to say anything? Are we going to drive around forever?" She knew it wouldn't be that, and she wasn't sure she wanted to hear his answer, but Rose was the kind of woman who would rather know the stakes than be surprised.

"I think we both know I can't drive us around forever, though I do think I'd enjoy your company. Eventually, if we can't have a polite conversation as I've suggested, there are other avenues we could take, figuratively speaking. I really don't think we'll need to do that, will we?"

Rose had been slowly slipping her phone from her purse, inch by inch while never looking down at it, hoping she could dial 911 without Malcolm seeing. "I'm sorry, Mrs. Conrad, but your phone will not work in here. I find phones are a bit of a nuisance when I'm conversing with someone. It feels a bit rude too. Don't you agree? So, though I respect how sly that was, I'm afraid a call isn't going to connect."

"I could press my face up to the window and scream. Maybe nobody hears me. But sooner or later someone will see an old lady screaming in the back seat of a car."

"Are you going to start screaming, Mrs. Conrad? That would really be unpleasant, and I don't think I'd be able to tolerate it for very long."

Rose slumped in her seat.

"See, you've already told me one thing, Mrs. Conrad. You've told me that there are secrets you want to keep. You wouldn't be so obstinate about sharing your conversation if there was nothing of interest."

"Or maybe I don't care for being kidnapped and threatened by my Uber driver."

"That also stands to reason, but I'd wager there's more to it. So, what did you and Matthew talk about?"

"Who are you? How do you know our names?" Rose asked.

"Mrs. Conrad, I know a lot of things. That's part of my job, you understand. What I don't know, or at least don't know the details of, is the conversation you and your grandson just had. Truth is, I will know that before too long too."

Rose clenched her teeth and shook her head slowly. "Stars Matty, what the hell did you stumble on?" She thought.

19

Crawford Notch

In roughly the center of White Mountain National Forest, there is a state park known as Crawford Notch. There is a parking area situated between Ripley Falls and the Webster-Jackson trailhead. This parking area is about a two-hour drive from Dover, a fact Matthew Conrad knew well. Thanks to his grandfather Cliff, he could get himself around the forest, find a place to park with or without a permit, and locate a desirable trail based on the season and prevailing weather conditions without a map or GPS.

It was not the careful selection of a trail that made Matthew drive two hours to Crawford Notch. It was a news story from three years prior. The Greathouse family; mother, father, and their two daughters had gone hiking on the Webster-Jackson trail. The article he'd read, and some of the sites where Matthew had seen them mentioned, suggested that they were not novice hikers. The girls, thirteen and fifteen, were experienced both on and off the trails. The parents had been hiking together most of their lives. They were a New Hampshire family.

Despite those facts, somewhere between the state park and surrounding national forest, Mrs. Greathouse went missing. The accounts Matthew read were cut and dry on the matter. Mr. Greathouse and his two daughters gave almost identical statements to the police and park officials. Mom was there, taking pictures of the horizon, and then she wasn't.

She hadn't wandered away. There was no gap in time when the family wasn't sure if maybe she'd stepped away, fallen, or taken a wrong turn. There were no sounds or signs of an animal attack. Search and rescue put in forty-eight hours and officially suspended the search.

Volunteers continued to hunt for the missing woman, but the focus quickly changed from tracking her whereabouts to an investigation of Mr. Greathouse. He'd become a suspect in his wife's murder. There were even allegations the girls were accomplices, or at least witnesses, to the father's alleged crime.

The case had attracted Matthew's attention for a few reasons. First, it was close to home. He could go see the area for himself, talk to the park rangers, and possibly contact the Greathouses. Second, he was intrigued by the short time search and rescue had looked before suspending the case and the rapid descent of the case into a murder investigation despite the lack of any evidence of foul play. Finally, he thought the Greathouse case might have been the one that Grandma Rose said Cliff had taken an interest in.

Mr. Greathouse was on record as saying, "She just vanished. I can't explain it, but there isn't any more to it." He was often interviewed by conspiracy websites and paranormal blog-writers but had grown tired of their spotlight and scrutiny, and after a year had removed himself from the public eye.

Matthew gathered photos he'd found online of where exactly Mrs. Greathouse had disappeared and was headed that direction. It was hard, as years passed, to find an exact location outdoors. Things grew and weathering and erosion changed the landscape. Ice storms took trees down and trails could be moved to account for changing terrain. But Matthew was fairly certain he could reconstruct their path.

The Greathouse family had parked in Crawford Notch and started hiking at the Webster-Jackson trailhead. Jennifer, the younger daughter, had told reporters they had walked off the trail maybe a hundred yards because they'd seen a family of deer and mom wanted to get a picture. Then, they lost sight of the deer, but they saw a spectacular horizon. So, they walked on a little further to get the best view, dad up front, then the girls, then mom. Isabelle, the older daughter, remembered her mother saying something about the light coming through trees and when she turned around to respond, mom was gone.

Matthew started along the trail and followed the notes, photos, and sketches he'd collected in his research. He found what he thought was the spot the family had left the trail. He headed into the woods, sweeping the ground for anything unusual like he'd seen in Utah.

At about a hundred and fifty yards, he heard a voice.

"You just don't listen, do you, Matty?"

Matthew looked up and saw Roger a few dozen yards down the trail, sitting on a tree stump.

"How the hell?"

"You leave a footprint. And you're predictable. That said, this place is remote and disconnected enough we might actually be able to have a conversation without worrying who's listening."

"Well, that would be a welcome change."

"Take a breath. I'm trying to help you."

"Are you? Because I can't tell what's helpful and what's a threat."

"I haven't threatened you. The Facebook messages and the note in the library were warnings. You are looking in some dangerous places, Matthew. You've poked around where you aren't supposed to. You went further than I told you... but that's my fault. I should have known you would. But now, you have The Order's attention and that's not the kind of attention you want."

"Wait. Before you go any further, are you telling me the whole of The Order is -"

"No. The *whole* of The Order doesn't get involved in anything. There are people within The Order, which means people inside damn near anything you can imagine, who have taken notice, who have been alerted to your inquiries."

"And what do they have to do with Rick's disappearance?"

"Nothing."

"Then why the hell am I looking into any of this?"

"I told you not to."

"And then you told me where to look."

"Because you weren't taking my warnings, and I wanted you to get some answers before you got hurt. Look, The Order didn't kidnap Rick. They didn't make him disappear, but they have a damn good idea what happened to him, and they want to be very sure they are the only ones who know what they know."

"How do you know all this?"

"I'm a member."

"Of The Order?"

"No, of the Mickey Mouse Club. Yes, The Order."

"Then you know about all the same stuff, don't you? You know the things they don't want people knowing."

"I also said that the entirety of The Order doesn't know about anything. They have dozens of areas of focus. What you're looking into wasn't one of mine, but I know enough about it to know they don't want you poking around. For god's sake look at what happened to the Greathouses; murder investigation instead of search and rescue, the media circus, reputations ruined, lives ruined. They worked so hard to make sure people were paying attention to father and daughters, talking about evidence, and motive, and dragging out all their dirty laundry people forget there was no sign of what happened to the mother at all."

"Wait, you're saying The Order-"

"Coordinates, influences, finances, supports, and corrupts with incredible speed and agility."

"I don't think they're going to put you in charge of recruiting," Matthew said.

"I haven't been an active member for years, but you're never really out."

"And why are you helping me? If this wasn't even your project, what's your interest?"

"If I understand what they're doing here, my interest is exposing them. These aren't all bad people, Matthew, but it is a breeding ground, or maybe just a fertile ground where bad things grow very rapidly. What you need to know is-"

"What I need to know is what they can tell me about my best friend. I need to know why people are going missing, where they are, and how I get them back."

"Those answers are out there. I'm living proof of some of those answers. I can't get your friend back. I'm not sure anyone can. You see-"

And that was it.

The last word from Roger's mouth was punctuated with a wet thump, a wisp of acrid smoke, and a spray of blood. Matthew felt frozen. He fell to his knees, unable to keep his legs from shaking, wiped the blood from his face onto his gloved hands, and stared at the gruesome visage of the strange man who'd turned his world inside out.

* * *

Had he taken the time to think about it, Matthew would have realized he had three options. First, he could have dropped to the ground, belly crawled behind the nearest solid object, like the tree stump that Roger had previously been sitting on and was now slumped backward over, and lay still, hoping that the gunman was only looking to kill one person that day.

Second, he could have dialed 911, reported as much as he could while huddling down in relative safety and hope the gunman had left. Third, he could have waited in place to see if the gunman was still in the area, then searched Roger for any clues or information he might be carrying.

Instead of choosing any of these options, Matthew ran. He catapulted deeper into the woods, which quickly gave way to a steep, rocky descent he had no choice but to run down, gravity and momentum deciding for him.

In retrospect, he would have preferred he spent his time running thinking about where he was going, thinking about who the gunman was, how he'd snuck up on them, how Roger had gotten to that spot before him. He would have preferred he'd spent the time running thinking of a plan, trying to decide what to do next, who to call, what to tell his family or the authorities, or which authorities to call.

Instead, his capacity for thinking was limited to three words, words which repeated over and over again as he picked up speed, "What the hell?"

Finally, gravity and momentum won the battle over balance and Matthew toppled, rolling several yards ungracefully, until he crashed into the trunk of a stately white pine. Righting himself, he sat propped against the tree, trying to catch his breath. The palms of his hands were torn, and he wiped a trickle of blood from his brow but felt no serious injury. He tried to calm his breathing enough to hear if someone approached.

"Of course," he thought, "I didn't hear the shooter approach in the first place."

Roger, or Woodrow Wilson, or whatever the hell his actual name was, was dead. All Matthew had got out of him was confirmation that people within The Order knew something about the disappearances, and they were aware of Matthew's search for answers. He knew Roger was a member, though clearly not one in good standing. He knew that, according to what had just happened, those in The Order with an interest in keeping what they knew a secret would go to great lengths to keep it that way.

Matthew patted the pockets of his jacket and discovered that neither his car keys nor his cell phone had fallen out in flight. The latter was still intact. He didn't have any signal in the valley as he had at the top of the rise, but he could still use the GPS to find his way back to the parking area. Then he realized he had dropped something, his grandfather's walking stick with the timepiece attached.

It had not been his plan to return to the grizzly scene at the tree stump. He was planning on heading back to his car, finding a place with good cell phone signal, and calling the park police, but he wasn't going anywhere without that walking stick.

Climbing back up took much longer than running down. His head was throbbing. His feet and knees ached. The scrape on his hand dripped blood. But Matthew persevered. Approaching the spot he was fairly he'd alighted from, he slowed to a crawl. Scanning the trees carefully and looking for any signs the shooter was still there, he inched closer.

He crawled to within sight of the tree stump where Roger should have been. There was no one there. There was no middle-aged man with a flat cap and a fresh hole in his head. There was no one on the ground. Matthew approached the stump and found there was not a drop of blood to be found.

He paced the area back and forth. He walked a spiral out from the stump, but there was absolutely no evidence anyone had been there. "Damn!" Matthew thought to himself. "Now what do I tell the authorities?"

He found his walking stick. Evidently, he'd lost his grip on it just as he started down the hill. It was laying in a patch of ferns a few dozen yards from the scene of the crime. Picking it up, he wiped some loose dirt from it, checked the timepiece was still intact, and put his hand through the leather cord at its top. "Now what, Grandpa?" He asked and desperately wished the man was there to reply.

Matt hiked back down the trail and returned to his car, wary someone might have him in their crosshairs. He watched. He listened. He tumbled through the same thoughts over and over.

"Now what?"

"What was Roger going to tell me?"

"Do I call the police?"

By the time he'd made it back to his car, he hadn't come up with answers. He had more questions.

"Was this a warning?"

"What had he meant about being living proof?"

"Was it about killing Roger or sending a message?"

Matthew called Dianne. Part of him wanted nothing more than to hear her voice, to feel grounded by her. Part of him knew that Dianne would have a fit, and rightfully so, about what had just happened. He needed her though. He needed her advice. So, he started the engine, turned on the heater, locked the doors, and pressed the speed-dial for Dianne.

20

Report

"Hey, I was just getting ready to call you! You remember that congressman I told you about?"

"They shot roger."

"Wait. What? You were with Roger? What do you mean they shot him? Where are you?"

"I'm outside of Conway, up near Crawford's."

"You went up there with Roger?"

"No. He was waiting for me when I got there."

"You didn't tell me you were going to meet him. Matthew, I'm a little pissed off you-"

"I didn't know he would be there, Dianne. I went to follow up on that story, the one I told you about the Greathouses."

"I know; the one I told you not to get wrapped up in. So, wait, he was there? He was shot? By who? Are you okay?"

"He'd started telling me about The Order. Dianne, there are people within The Order who know about the disappearances, who probably know about Rick. They know something about the Greathouses. Roger was just starting to tell me about it, and he was shot. Someone shot him between the eyes."

"Oh Jesus! Did you see the shooter? Are you okay? Did you call the police?"

Matthew recounted his flight, his return for the walking stick, and the cleaned-up crime scene. "There was no body! Dianne, there wasn't a sign anyone had been there."

Dianne asked more than once if Matthew was sure he'd been in the right place, and Matthew pointed out he wouldn't have found the walking stick if he'd been in the wrong place. She began wondering, not for the first time if her partner was coming unglued. Was it possible he'd imagined it? She didn't want to think Matthew had been so traumatized he was coming apart, but the signs were there.

"Matthew. I want you to come home. You get a cup of tea in Conway somewhere and you come home to me, okay?"

"Okay. Should I call the police?"

"I'm not sure. Let me think about it. My head is probably a little clearer than yours. You focus on coming home safe."

"Okay. I'm sorry, honey. Obviously, I had no idea this was going to-"

"I know. You have nothing to apologize for. Just come home."

Dianne pressed ended the call. Linda was looking over her shoulder. "What the shit Dianne?"

Dianne hadn't told her office-mate much about Matthew's recent activity. She decided to then because she needed someone to talk to. "Hang on. I'll fill you in in just a second. I need to make another call."

Dianne dialed Grandma Rose's number, knowing that she was likely the most well suited to help her sort out what Matthew was going through. The number rang several times and then an automated voice informed her that Grandma Rose hadn't set up her voice mail.

Linda wheeled her chair over to Dianne's desk, tipped a fresh pot of coffee into Dianne's waiting mug, and plopped down in the chair. "Spill," she said.

Dianne filled Linda in on everything that had transpired with Matthew since she had returned from Utah. She included every detail she could, as objectively as she could, saving the editorializing until she was finished and the two of them could do it together.

"And that," she concluded the story by indicating her phone sitting on the corner of her desk, "was Matthew calling to tell me that his trip to the mountains to look into an old missing person's cases ended with him witnessing a murder."

Linda's mouth gaped. She began a reply a couple of times and then trailed off.

"Linda, I honestly don't know if Matt is in the middle of something serious and dangerous or if he's cracking up. He loved Rick and now Rick is gone. Maybe this is him dealing with the trauma, you know… his mind has invented some conspiracy story. But seeing someone get killed? That's really ramping up the trauma response."

"Unless it isn't. What if it's real? I mean seriously! Weird shit happens all over the place, all the time. What if Matt just happened to stumble onto something he shouldn't have, and this really is as intense as he says it is? Di, someone was just shot. You really think Matt would make that up?"

"Not intentionally, no. But what if he believes it's happening and it isn't?"

Linda rocked back in her office chair, chewed on a wooden coffee stirrer for a moment, and said, "I've only met Matt a few times. I mean, I've seen him when he's come in to visit you, but really only met him to talk a few times. The impression I got was of a totally down to Earth dude. Everything you've ever told me suggests that."

"Down to Earth people lose it too, Linda."

"Don't take this wrong way, Di, but I think you want to think he's crazy because the alternative is he's gotten himself, and therefore you, into some major shit."

Dianne said nothing. She pursed her lips. Then, she chewed lightly at her lower lip, part of her wishing she still smoked because this was exactly the right kind of moment for lighting up.

"You okay?" Linda asked.

"What if you're right?"

"Well…"

"I mean, what… how do we even begin? When I thought this was a prank, it annoyed me. I was getting ready to call the police, but how do I deal with this now?" Dianne asked.

"Are you going to call the police?"

"Not before Matt gets back and we talk about it. Do you think I should?"

"Honey, I have no idea."

* * *

"I'd like to report a crime."

The phone call had started simply enough. He and Dianne had discussed it as Matthew unwound by alternately pacing the floor and sitting on the couch holding her hand.

"No, it isn't a crime in progress, and it is not at my current location."

The expression on Matthew's face, even after having the two-hour drive home to talk himself down, pushed Dianne fully into the "some serious stuff is going on" camp.

"Jackson-Webster trail, north of Crawford Notch State Park in the White Mountains," Matthew said.

If whatever was going on was at a level where people could die being involved in it, it was not something Dianne wanted them to handle it on their own. They had decided to call the state police.

"I was hiking, and I came across a body. Someone had been shot. It was a middle-aged man, maybe early sixties. He was wearing a three-quarter length, tan overcoat and had a gray flat cap on. There was a wound in his head. No, no one else was around. No, you are the first phone call I made. Yes, ma'am. I called as soon as I had signal and was safely off the road. Two hours ago."

He gave his contact information, described as best he could where Roger could be found, and left out all details that could connect Matthew to the recently deceased. The dispatch operator said she would send someone to take a full statement and would contact Park Police to follow up. It all felt very routine until the state troopers arrived.

"Mr. Conrad, I'm Officer Mendez. This is Officer Carlton. We're with the New Hampshire State Police." He flashed a badge, though given his attire; it wasn't necessary. "May we come in?"

Matt introduced Dianne, who offered to make a pot of coffee. Officer Mendez politely accepted.

"Mr. Conrad," the latter began. "I've been in touch with park police and troopers in Crawford Notch. There are things from your phone call that aren't adding up. Why don't you tell us what happened in the mountains from the time you arrived?"

Matthew, impatient and nervous, walked Office Mendez through arriving at the park, hiking into the woods, and invented the part where he came across a body slumped over on a tree stump.

Mendez asked, "And, can you tell us again exactly what time it was when you came across this body?"

Matthew went back through his story, estimating times as well as he could, including what time he'd made it back to the car. He almost used his phone log to verify what time he'd called Dianne, but was afraid of highlighting the fact that over two hours had passed between his departure and calling the police.

"And what did you say brought you to that particular place in the woods? Park Police told us it was well off the trail."

"I didn't say, actually. But since you ask, I was looking around a place where a woman went missing a little while back. I'd read the story on a hiking blog and was curious."

"A trip all the way out there just for that?" Carlton asked.

"No. I was out there to hike the trail but stopped by that area while I was up there."

"I see," Mendez said, adding notes to his pad.

"Here is where we come into a problem, Mr. Conrad. Officers have searched the area you describe. There is no body. There is no blood, nor any sign of a struggle. There's no sign of anyone having been there."

"What?"

"No body, Mr. Conrad. There is nothing there. Filing a false police report, especially over something like finding a body, well that's a serious crime you know."

"I'm not doing that. I'm not filing anything false. I saw a guy with a hole in his head, slumped across a tree stump. It freaked me out. I came home, and I called you, or I called the station or dispatch or whatever."

"I see," Carlton said.

"Listen, Mr. Conrad, we will continue to investigate this. I will need you to stay in the area. I need some additional contact information so we can locate you at work, for example. I will also want your... roommate's information."

"That's my girlfriend. I'll give you her information."

Matthew realized that in the entire time they'd been talking, Dianne had not returned with the coffee. He also didn't hear her in the kitchen.

"That's okay. We'll get it. Where did she go?"

"Dianne!" Matt yelled.

Dianne walked slowly in from the other room, her face drawn, a startled look in her eyes. Matt cocked his head at her, and she subtly shook her hers. "I'm sorry officers," she said, "I never did get your coffee. I suddenly wasn't feeling very well. If I had any to-go cups, I'd pour you some for the road."

"Thanks for the thought," Carlton said. "We're about done here. Trooper Mendez had a few things he needs to ask you. Then we'll be on our way." Carlton was transferring notes to a long form attached to a clipboard he'd laid across his lap.

Having completed their business, Mendez and Carlton walked to the door. They thanked Matt and Dianne for their time and left.

Dianne immediately turned to Matthew and said, "She's okay, and she's back home, but they got to your grandmother, Matt. They got to her this afternoon. What the hell is going on?"

21

Determination

"Grandma! Are you okay?"

"Yes, dear. I'm okay; a little rattled is all. I hope Dianne filled you in. I'm too tired to go over it again."

"Yes, she did. You're sure you're okay?"

Grandma Rose took a deep breath, sighed, and said, "Matty, I think he was going to… get rid of me if I didn't tell him. I don't know what he would have done. I had to tell him. I had to. I'm sorry, Matthew."

"I know. Dianne told me."

"She told me the police were there. She said someone got shot. Are you okay?"

"Yeah. Yeah, I think so. I was giving a statement when you called. Dianne filled you in?"

"I think I got the big picture. Are you in trouble with the police, Matthew?"

"I don't know. I don't think so. They told us to stick around the area, which we were planning on anyway. I'm sure we'll hear from them again. Get some rest, grandma. I'll call you tomorrow."

"You got it, kiddo."

"And please don't go anywhere," he added.

"You bet your ass I won't. I love you, Matty."

"I love you too, grandma."

* * *

"Matt, this is obviously not a hoax. I'm sorry. I-"

"Don't worry about it. You see it now. A man was killed. Then his body disappears. An Uber driver kidnapped and interrogated my grandmother, and I am absolutely no closer to having any idea what's going on, never mind any closer to knowing what happened to Rick."

"What are you going to do?"

"I don't know."

"Are you going to keep digging, Matt? I think this is significant enough you can't. Your grandmother was in danger. They've killed someone."

"I don't know. I can't bear the thought of anyone I love getting hurt. At the same time, if whatever I've stumbled on, whatever Roger was trying to tell me is important enough to hide, then it's probably something that shouldn't be hidden."

"Even if that's true, what can you do about it? It seems like Roger was your only clue, and someone was willing to execute him to shut him up."

"Why didn't they shoot me?" Matt asked flatly.

"What?"

"I'm the one asking the questions. Why didn't they shoot me? And for that matter, why wait until I was there to shoot Roger? They had to have been watching him. The shooter let us talk for a couple minutes before he pulled the trigger. Why?"

"I don't know, but you clearly have an idea."

"It was a warning. It was their way of telling me to back off."

"Hell of a warning. Maybe it was less about you than this Roger character. Someone didn't want him saying any more than he already had."

"Maybe. I think grandma was a way of finding out what I knew. It was also to show me how close they can get."

"Are you going to take those warnings, Matt?"

"I don't know."

Dianne slumped back against the back of the couch and sighed, knowing her partner's "I don't know," was as good as an admission he wasn't walking away.

Matt said, "I don't know what the right thing to do is, but I know people are going missing, and if someone knows how or why, don't I owe it to the families of those missing people to pursue it as far as I can? Don't I owe it to Rick, to Martha?"

"You owe it to yourself. Is that part of this, Matt? Is it guilt? I know you think you're responsible, but you aren't. And getting yourself, or your grandmother or me killed won't bring Rick back, and it isn't going to bring you closure."

"I know it isn't. But maybe if I can figure out what's going on... if I can... change it, maybe I can help bring closure to the families of the others. Maybe it will bring some kind of peace to the people they left behind."

22

Rick

He had been treated kindly, and that was something. It hadn't been like the police station where rough handling and dour, suspicious stares appeared to be the norm. It wasn't as though he were an honored guest either. Rick considered he still had no firm grasp on what was happening to him, but he no longer felt as though he had broken with reality.

There was a knock on his door, a gesture of politeness before a man entered. This was not a police officer, nor was it a man in a hazmat suit. This man had a professorial look, khaki pants, a comfortable-looking sweater, and round, thin-framed glasses. He smiled at Rick and indicated the chair in the corner of the room near the foot of the bed. "Do you mind?"

Rick nodded his head, although he was certain whether he minded made no difference. "Mr. Minor, I have read through your file, that is to say over the transcripts of your interview with the police and the conversations you've had with personnel at this facility."

"If you want to call them conversations."

"Indeed," the man said. "It's clear, based on all the evidence we have, you do not know where you are or how you got here."

"I've said that several times."

"I understand, but I need *you* to understand this is something we must establish with a high degree of certainty."

"Why?"

"I'll get to that in due course. My name is Dr. Schreiber. I have the distinction of helping you understand where you are, but I have found over the years it is far easier to hear it from someone from… of similar origins."

"Doc., I have no idea what that means. You said 'years?'"

"Yes, Rick. May I call you Rick? Yes, I have been at this almost my entire career."

"At what?"

"At the business of understanding 'the people who appear.' Are you familiar with the term?"

Rick rubbed his face with the palm of his hand. "Uh, yeah, I've heard it. Are you saying-"

Dr. Schreiber rose from his chair and opened the door. "Would you care to follow me, please?"

Rick rose. "Are you saying 'the people who appear' are a real… thing?"

Instead of answering, Dr. Schreiber said, "There is a security officer who will follow us, but please do not be alarmed. It's a standard protocol for all government buildings. Frankly, I'd be more concerned if there wasn't a guard at every corner."

He indicated for Rick to exit the room, then joined him and the security guard and led them down the hall. "I'll introduce you to Annie. Annie arrived here several years ago. She left our facility after about twelve weeks but found difficulty acclimating, so she's in a transitional place at the moment. I'll let her fill you in. I've prepared a conference room for you, although we've tried to make it feel more like a modern living room. You'll be free to chat, but naturally, since you are in a government facility, you can expect your conversation will be monitored and recorded."

"Not exactly 'free to talk' then is it?"

"Do you have secrets to keep? Do you know Annie or expect that she will have secrets to keep?"

Rick shook his head.

"Then you should have nothing to worry about by being monitored."

Dr. Schreiber opened the door and ushered Rick inside. The guard who had followed them down the hall nodded to another guard stationed outside the room, then returned to stand outside the room Rick had been in.

As soon as Rick took a step past the door frame, he was nearly bowled over by a charging bear hug from a stout, middle-aged woman in a floral dress. Dr. Schreiber seemed unaffected. He smiled at Annie, and Annie smiled back to him. "I'll be back in a little while, Annie. I'm sure Rick has a lot of questions."

"Thanks, hon," Annie replied and turned to Rick, "I'm sorry. I just... it's not often... I rarely get to meet or even see someone from the other side."

"The other side?"

"Sit, sugar. The couches they scrounged up for us are pretty comfy actually, and there's a coffee maker and a tea kettle if you're interested." She gestured to a small counter along the far wall.

"How about whiskey?"

Annie smiled and shook her head. "Sorry, hon."

"Thanks anyway." Rick crossed the little room and sat on the edge of one of the couches with his elbows resting on his knees. "You said 'the other side?'"

"I suppose it's the best place to jump in." Annie smiled, gave a little sigh, and sat on the second couch. "The Other Side is just a name some of us use to differentiate where we are now and where we used to be."

"You may have to back up a little for me, Annie."

"Okay. So, you haven't been here very long, I take it. You haven't seen or heard enough to make any sense of this, have you?"

"I've been here long enough to know I'm not in Kansas anymore."

Annie grinned from ear to ear. She chuckled softly to herself and then, to Rick's surprise, wiped a tear from the corner of her eye. "I'm sorry, Rick. I just haven't heard that in a long time. No one here would have the slightest idea what it meant. There aren't as many differences as you might think, but the *Wizard of Oz* was actually a dud here. They don't even keep it in their video library... their loss."

She stood back up and crossed to the electric tea kettle on the counter. "Okay, so I can't tell you exactly whether you're in another place as we think of places. I can't tell you if you're in another dimension as Rod Serling might have put it. All I can tell you for certain is this is not the United States of America you and I know. It's not the world we know. Somehow reality is different here."

"I've gathered that."

"Where we're from, people vanish. I don't mean they run away from home, or go off the grid, or anything like that. I mean, they actually vanish. At least that's what it looks like from *that* side. But you didn't vanish, Rick, because here you are. You came through some kind of... door... a passage to this when and where."

"And you did too?"

"I did. As far as I can tell it's been a couple of years now. Let me ask you, was it from a park?"

Rick's eyes went wide. "Why would you guess that?"

"I've met several us and there is a disproportionate number who come from national parks and other public lands."

"Why is that?"

"People have their theories."

"What's yours?"

"Well, I don't know that I have my own, but I can tell you the people in this building are awfully cautious about it. That's why you were so thoroughly checked out. My understanding is people on this side know there's another side. They didn't realize things were slipping through. And there is a contingent who believes we've been purposely sent here, and not necessarily with the best of intentions."

Rick looked puzzled and said, "That's ridiculous. I was hiking with some friends in a park in Utah and the next thing I know I'm... I'm here and not a damn thing makes any sense."

"I was picking flowers. I know. I know. You aren't supposed to pick flowers from the parks. Trust me, I've learned my lesson. But, well, like I said, it's just a theory some people have."

"You mentioned others? Where are they? Are they all in this building?"

"No. A lot of them are in group homes, halfway houses you might call them. A few have gone on to really live here; assimilate you might say. And some, well, some are still trying to find their way back."

"And you?"

Annie breathed deep and then pursed her lips. "It wasn't for me. I… it's too much out there. I never could adjust to the differences. But you will. You get situated, get your head around it, and I'm sure you'll be just fine."

"I'm not sure I want to be 'just fine.' I want to go home."

"That's true for us all, I imagine, hon. But I'm afraid that's easier said than done."

"Can't we just find the… the doors we slipped through and go back to the other side, back to where we came from?"

"I don't know if we can go back through or not. You'd have to find the doorways first. It's not like we saw where they were when we came through to this side." Annie's lips were lightly pursed, her head tilted slighted downward.

"But, people go missing from this place too, right? I mean, they must."

"Sure. But there's no way of knowing if they slipped through back to our world or not, just like there's no way for the people probably looking for you to know you're anywhere but lost in the woods."

"You said people on this side know there's another side though."

"Government people, yes. It seems that way."

"So they'd know if people can cross both ways, wouldn't they?"

"I don't know. I just know that much about it, Rick. For now, for today at least, I think you need to try to process the part about being in another world, another reality. Save the questions about getting home for another time."

23

The Note

"Grandma, I am so sorry I've gotten you wrapped up in this. I had no idea."

"I know, Matty. You couldn't have known this would happen. You couldn't have. You'd never knowingly do anything that would put me or anyone else in danger."

"No. Of course not."

"You needed to talk, and I have always been, and will always be, someone you can talk to."

Matthew asked, "Are you hurt?"

"No. I'm a little shaky today, but nothing I can't manage."

"Did you tell mom and dad about what happened?" Matthew asked.

"No, but it took a bit of convincing your dad I was just enjoying time at the senior center and that's why I got home later than expected. Matthew, are you okay?"

"I am. I guess I'm a little shaky too."

"I'll say. It's not every day someone sees what you saw." Matthew couldn't help but notice her reluctance to say, "see a man get killed." She was probably too unnerved to say it out loud.

"No, that's for sure. And then to be visited by a couple of state troopers looking at me like I'm crazy or making things up… Long day. For sure. What did this Uber driver ask you about?"

"Like I told Dianne, honey, he wanted to know what you knew, or at least what you had told me about your search for these missing people. Talk about convincing. I don't know how many times I had to repeat I didn't know much. I told him you were searching for clues. I told him you'd stumbled onto some conspiracy theory involving a secret organization. I said I didn't know the details, but he wouldn't believe me. Matthew, I told them everything you told me. I didn't know what else to do. I'm sorry if I screwed up."

"You did fine, Grandma. Telling the truth was probably for the best."

"I hope so, kiddo. I just hate to think I've put you in any danger. I told them about this man you'd been in touch with." There was a pause, then, "Jesus Matthew, did I get that man killed?"

"No. No, grandma. I don't think so. It must have all happened at the same time. There's no way what you told the Uber driver could have gotten to the shooter in time for him to track us down... or track him down and shoot him."

"Damn, Matty. I was trying not to say that part. I mean, I was trying to be vague and all. You know the phone is probably tapped; my end, your end, both? Hi Malcolm," she said. "Thanks for not killing an innocent old lady for talking to her grandson. Asshole."

Matt couldn't help but snicker. He'd never heard his grandmother use that term before. She chuckled a little too, then she said, "You listen to me, Matthew. You do what you think is right. Don't worry about your grandma or your parents, not for one minute. We'll be fine. Your grandfather taught your father and me how to take care of ourselves. And doing the right thing, no matter what, was your grandfather's way. I can't tell you what the right thing is. That's on you. Follow your gut, but don't let worrying about us influence your choices."

Matt didn't think it was possible not to worry about them or how to not let his concern for them factor into his decision-making. "Thanks, grandma. I appreciate it. I love you."

"I know, kiddo. I love you too. You take care of yourself. Oh, and call your mother sometime soon. I heard her saying something to your dad the other day about you not checking in with them."

"You got it. Take care."

"Of course. You too."

"I'll try." He ended the call.

Matthew had needed to know she was okay. He wasn't worried so much about what grandma had told the Malcolm as he was that she was okay, and of course, she was. Grandma Rose was made of the same stuff as the New Hampshire mountains, granite through and through.

Matt had also wanted, perhaps needed, her to endorse his continuing his search. He knew it's what she would do. He knew she would tell him to follow his gut and do the right thing, and she knew him well enough to know that as far as he was concerned, "the right thing," was to keep looking.

Having spoken to her and reassured himself she wasn't hurt and had firm footing beneath her, Matthew felt ready to start the day. It was difficult, he discovered, to pretend at normal, to follow normal routines, or go about the everyday tasks of life when your life was saturated with the abnormal.

* * *

"Cummings. DOI. Leadership. -DL"

The letter, if that's what it could be called, had arrived not in the mailbox at Matt and Dianne's Dover address but in his in-basket at school, having been placed there while he was away from his desk presumably by the mailroom clerk, Stacy. He'd seen her moving her cart through the library while he was in the stacks. It was there, sandwiched between a manila, interoffice envelope he hadn't bothered to open yet, and an invitation to a lecture in Richmond he was not the least bit interested in. Mail deliveries were sparse in the age of digital communications.

The note was handwritten on a small strip of plain white paper. The envelope was unremarkable; letter-sized, addressed to him at the school, no return address. It bore a standard "forever" stamp. Rick noticed that it hadn't been postmarked. He hadn't noticed that until after he read it and returned to the envelope looking for some kind of clue.

As a young man alive in the internet age was prone to do, Matt's first step had been to open a browser and type in the exact text from the note. "Cumming. DOI. Leadership." He omitted the "D.L." as it appeared to be a signature, though he wasn't certain whose signature it was.

The web search returned immediately intriguing results. John Alan Cummings was the deputy secretary of the Department of the Interior. Matthew wasn't especially familiar with the myriad departments in the executive branch of the United States government, but he knew that one. The National Parks Service was nested under the DOI. As the deputy secretary, J.A. Cummings qualified as "leadership."

Matthew felt his pulse quicken. He read the short bio on the department's "Who We Are" page. Then he turned to Wikipedia and read up on J.A. Cummings. There wasn't anything startling in it. He appeared to be a lifetime politician, starting as a republican representative from Texas. Not surprisingly, he was also named as a member of The Order. There was nothing written in the entry specifically about his involvement in The Order, it was simply listed as one of his affiliations.

Seeing nothing else of genuine interest, Matthew read and re-read the note, making sure there weren't any clues buried "between the lines."

When he had first opened the envelope and found the scrap of paper, his initial thought had been it was a last message from Roger, but "D.L.," didn't fit. Nor were D.L. the initials of any dead presidents. Matthew slipped his phone out of his pocket and sent Dianne a text message.

"Got a clue today. Note arrived in the mailbox from D.L. Might need your help."

It took a few minutes, Matthew obsessively checking his phone before he received a reply. "D.L.? What kind of help."

"Don't know. Will discuss at lunch?"

This time the reply was almost immediate. "Actress. Can't make it. My office?"

"Actress?" Matthew thought. "What does-" and then it struck him, and he chastised himself for not getting it immediately. "Danielle Lovejoy."

"Right! And yes." He texted back to Dianne. Followed by, "Love you. Thanks." It took substantial discipline for Matthew to focus on the rest of the morning's work. All his mind wanted to do was race ahead to Dianne or process what the deputy secretary of the Department of the Interior might know about the people missing from "his" parks. Matthew also kept an eye on his desk any time he wandered away from it, having developed a paranoia something or someone might appear while he wasn't looking.

24

The Capital

"I was thinking," Matthew said, "It might make more sense to go to his office than to try to contact him."

"More sense?" Dianne asked. After she had spoken to Rose the night before, she had been trying to approach all the strangeness in their lives as their new reality and approach Matthew's discoveries objectively. It was easier said than done.

"As much as any of it makes sense," he said. "It's easy to avoid someone's emails or phone calls. It gets a little harder if you're in their face."

"Okay, but how do you propose to get in the deputy secretary of the Department of the Interior's face?"

"I haven't worked that out yet," Matt shrugged and took another bite of his steak and cheese sub. He tried to eat vegetarian most of the time. It wasn't his preference, but he felt strongly about supporting Dianne. It was a matter of solidarity. That afternoon, however, he needed a little comfort food. His stomach would likely not appreciate it, but Dianne had said nothing. She understood. "I suppose the first step is to go to D.C.."

Dianne stopped crunching at her salad for a moment and swallowed hard. "Just show up in D.C.? What about work? You've already used all your time, haven't you?" She knew very well he had.

"Yes. But there are always conferences and symposiums going on run by the Library of Congress and some of the universities there. I'm sure I could find something the department would give me professional leave to attend."

"And you'd make stalking Cummings a side trip?"

"No, I'd make it the whole trip."

Dianne shook her head and took another forkful of her salad.

"I... I was thinking we'd both go," Matthew said.

"What? Matthew, I have classes and things are going on at Earth Action I need to take care of. The bill Congressman Sperling was talking about is in congressional review, and I've just started putting together a campaign."

Matt smiled sheepishly, "Well, I was thinking it would be a great opportunity for you to meet Mr. Sperling. Make an appointment to visit him so you can talk strategy."

Dianne smirked, shook her head again, and said, "You've thought this through, haven't you?"

"A little."

* * *

Congressman Sperling's office scheduled Dianne an appointment early the next week. Matt was pleased because it gave him time to find the right cover story and sell it to his superiors at the university. Dianne was glad to have a few days to finish her campaign proposals, reach out to her contacts, and rally support before leaving.

She was organizing marches in several cities across the US and wanted to show the congressman how quickly she could mobilize people. Meanwhile, they had agreed, or perhaps Dianne had convinced Matthew he should suspend or at least severely limit his investigation. They didn't want anything more complicated to deal with before leaving for, or while they were in, Washington. Dianne had also used the argument that if Matthew looked like he had backed off, then the powers at play might assume the incidents with Roger and Grandma Rose had been successful.

Matthew, unable to focus on his work, had started imagining what his meeting with J.A. Cummings was apt to be like. He assumed he would be able to get to see the man, though he'd had to conjure scenarios where he ambushed the politician at a cafe or bar or followed him to his office. "The head of the cabal," was what he'd begun calling Cummings, and he was increasingly certain that if he could pin the man down, he could get answers.

Having exhausted their travel budget in Utah, Matt and Dianne were forced to drive to D.C.. It should have been an eight-hour drive, but with traffic it had ended up closer to ten. Matthew was quickly reminded why he enjoyed New Hampshire.

The drive was subdued. Matthew asked about Earth Action's campaign and Dianne had been more than happy to share everything she'd thought about, everything she would try to do, and the work Linda would be doing while Dianne was away.

Once they had exhausted that topic, a quiet fell over the car. Matthew didn't want to talk, didn't want to speculate about how his part of the trip would unfold. He'd noticed that Dianne was not resisting his search anymore, but he didn't want to push it. He knew she was worried about his safety and probably her own, and he didn't want to put her on edge in the face of what, for her, was a legitimate business trip.

"Did you tell your parents you were headed out of town?" She asked.

"Yeah. I called this morning before we left. I told them there was a work thing and you had an appointment. I didn't get into it. Dad said to wish you 'good luck' by the way. Mom thought it was nice we were getting out of town." He didn't mention the list of places his mother suggested as romantic locations to propose while they were there.

They'd found an inexpensive hotel and arrived around their usual dinner time but decided to wait a couple of hours before venturing out, reasoning they would battle even worse traffic at that time of the day. Dianne opened her laptop on the little round table in the hotel room and checked her email. Matt tried to take a nap, but couldn't settle his mind enough. So, he lay on the bed and continued quietly practicing to himself what he would say to Cummings.

* * *

Matt and Dianne rode the Metro to Capitol South Station and walked the Capitol building. Matt walked Dianne up the steps and gave her a kiss, wishing her luck. He proudly watched her enter the building, then he set off towards C Street.

He had considered walking the entire way. It was a good chance for a pleasant stroll and there was plenty to see, but he'd decided if Dianne finished before he did, he didn't want to keep her waiting and wasn't sure how long he'd be.

He'd been able to make an appointment to meet a woman from the National Parks Service under the auspices of research for the university. He had his school-employee ID badge strung on a lanyard around his neck. That got him in the door; gave him a reason to be there. The rest would demand thinking on his feet.

Matt boarded the nearest Metro. The Department of the Interior office was nearer the White House than it was the Capitol. It wasn't a long ride, but it was not nearly as pleasant as being above ground, in the open air with sights to see.

He arrived early and wandered the halls as far as security would allow. He was looking for the office of J.A. Cummings, which he assumed would be large and prominently situated, or for the man himself, having looked at enough pictures online to be sure he would recognize him. Minutes before the meeting was scheduled, when he should have been sitting professionally and patiently in one of the padded chairs outside the Parks Department's office, he spotted Cummings exiting a room down the hall and heading around a corner.

Matthew shot to his feet and called, "Mr. Cummings! A word, please!"

The deputy secretary turned to look at him. He was an usually tall man, sturdily built with close-cropped, light brown hair. He was clean-shaven and had sharp green eyes. "I'm sorry. Do you have an appointment?" He called down the hallway.

"I have one with the parks' office, but I was hoping to catch you for a quick word while I'm here."

"I'm sorry. I'm a very busy man. I would be happy to discuss whatever it is you need to talk about, just not now. Please stop in and see my secretary." He turned again and stepped another few paces down the hall, fishing his phone out of the pocket of his slacks when Matthew called again.

"It's about Woodrow Wilson… about Roger."

Cummings stopped and turned around. "What did you say?"

"I said it's about Roger. He contacted me under the name Woodrow Wilson. We've spoken several times. He came to see me in New Hampshire."

"I don't have any idea what you're talking about."

"You do though," Matthew insisted. "If not you, then someone in this office."

"I'm sorry," Cummings said. "I don't know who you're referring to."

"Roger was in The Order. You know that. I think you know exactly who I'm talking about. It was a member of The Order who told me to find you."

"Sir, a lot of people are in The Order. It's no secret. I am a proud member myself. Now, I'm afraid I have to ask you to leave. Without an appointment, I don't have time to speak with you, and I am disinclined to discuss whatever or whoever you're talking about. If you do not leave of your own accord, I will call security, who will in turn contact the D.C. police."

Matthew knew he was running out of time. He didn't have a lot of cards to play, but this was likely his only shot at DOI leadership. Cummings was turning the corner. "You can't just make me disappear. People don't just vanish!" he called at Cummings, hoping what was between the lines was clear.

Cummings turned and walked briskly towards him. "Let's go into my office, shall we?" He opened the door he'd exited earlier and held it for Matthew who stepped inside. He remained standing while Cummings walked around the stately, polished desk and sat, the ankle of one leg resting across the knee of the other. He steepled his fingers and stared silently at Matthew for a moment.

"I don't know what you think you know," he said, "But I assure you, you're chasing phantoms. You aren't the first person to come through here with mad ideas about clandestine organizations and conspiracies. You're just the first looking for me specifically. I brought you in here so you didn't make a scene in the hallway and embarrass us both. I will suggest you gather your wits, take a breath, and forget whatever wild goose chase you're on. Then you should leave."

"You don't deny you're in The Order?"

"No. As I said, I'm a proud member of a time-honored fraternal organization."

"Do you deny knowledge of unsolved missing persons cases on federal lands?"

"No. I don't keep apprised of all of them. That would be the park's office, as I'm sure you know. I am also aware of several wild theories regarding how these people come to be missing. I assure you there is nothing to them."

"Do you know the man Roger, who used the pseudonym Woodrow Wilson?"

"Does Roger have a last name?"

"I'm not sure that Roger is even really his first name. I do know that he has tried to direct me on some research into the disappearances. I know he claimed to be a member of The Order, although not one in good standing. And I know that I saw him shot between the eyes in the White Mountain National Forest."

Cummings didn't reply. He sat with his jaw clenched, staring fixedly at a point in space somewhere over Matthew's right shoulder.

"That's right," Matthew continued. "A man was killed; a man who had followed me into the mountains to tell me about the connection between the national parks and disappearances, to tell me about the connection between the parks and The Order. A day after he was killed, I received an anonymous note giving me your name. You know more than you're saying, Mr. Cummings, and one way or another I will find out what it is."

That shook the man out of his gaze. "What? Is that supposed to be some kind of threat? 'One way or another?' What are you going to do to pry secrets you think I have out of me? One of us is what, a grad student from New Hampshire?" he waved a finger derisively at Matthew's university ID badge, "And the other is a cabinet-level, presidentially appointed deputy secretary in a federal department who also happens to a member of one of the oldest and most well-connected organizations in the nation. What are you going to do?"

"I'm going to..." Matt didn't know what he would do. He did know he would not be bullied, not when he might be within arm's reach of understanding what had happened to his best friend, what had happened to all the other missing people. "I'm going to make as public a spectacle as you've ever seen," he said, having no idea how we going to accomplish that.

"And who will take you seriously? You're going to make a spectacle out of some outlandish theory that the Parks Department is what, covering up disappearances? That the Department of the Interior is complicit in human abduction? Whatever your theory is, no one will listen to it. You'll be written off as a nut, your story relegated to obscure blogs, then forgotten. The closest you'll come to a public spectacle is a group of stoner undergrads dreaming up a documentary."

"I have more resources than you know." Matt began raising his voice, fighting to keep calm so his words came from reason and not emotion, but his proximity to this man, a man who might have answers was driving his blood pressure up by the minute. "My best friend went missing. My grandmother was kidnapped and interrogated. A man was executed in front of me. You think I'll give up that easily?"

Cummings stood, leaned towards Matthew, his fingertips pressed to his desk. "You think you have resources? If any of this is true, if we could get to your dear granny, or send an assassin into the mountains to hunt down your 'deep throat,' don't you think we have the resources to make you disappear before you could be any kind of nuisance for us? I'm sorry you are not coping well with your loss, Mr. Conrad, but I suggest you find a healthier way to manage it than coming to Washington D.C. and threatening a cabinet official. I'll thank you to exit my office and this building quietly and this building quietly. Go back to Dover. Live your life." Rather than rise and show Matthew out like he'd shown him in, Cunnings sat back down and pointed to the door.

Matthew scowled at him, but was at a loss for anything more to say. His anger fought for dominance with his disappointment. He had no more information than he'd had before he arrived. He felt a pang of rising guilt that he was no closer to justice. He walked out of the office, pulling the door closed behind him, and walked towards the exit. He paused a moment just before leaving the building.

The thought struck him he'd never told Cummings where in New Hampshire he lived, and yet the man had said "Dover."

25

Conflict of Interest

Across town, Dianne was sitting with Democratic representative Sperling discussing the president's proposed budget cuts and their effects on federal lands. Not only would conservation and preservation funds be cut, but there was the suggestion that the size of several parks would be reduced, some eliminated, and it would make these lands available to natural gas and oil exploration.

The congressman appeared impressed with the number of people ready to mobilize Dianne had already been in contact with. Their conversation centered on whether it was better to mount an information and awareness campaign or a physical protest. Dianne brought press clippings from Earth Action's "Save the Bay" efforts, which the congressman had already seen, citing them as the reason he'd contacted her.

"At this stage," Dianne said, "I think we need to be visible. There are so many petitions out there, such a clutter of information and disinformation, it's hard to be heard through the noise. If that's what you want Earth Action to do, we could find a way to make that kind of campaign stand out, but if this is a budget that's already made it to review, people need to know now. They need to be seen and heard."

"I agree. This is a bill that cannot pass."

Dianne appreciated the congressman's dedication to environmental issues. Her research into his voting record and political history in Colorado seemed to illustrate a passion for preservation. Given the natural beauty of the state, she wasn't surprised, but there was something steely in his tone when he referred to *this* bill which raised the hackles on her neck. She couldn't put her finger on it. She also couldn't stop thinking about Matthew and the conversation he might be having in the DOI at that very moment.

"I agree, this budget cannot pass," she said. "Can I ask though, what is so different about this budget? I understand it's a lot of land we're talking about, but there have been other budgets like it."

"And I have stood against every one."

"I know. I didn't mean to imply otherwise. You are clearly passionate about this one in particular. Is there some personal significance to the lands in question?"

"No, and if there was, we'd leave it out of the conversation. If there was a personal connection, the opposition would latch on to it and it would weaken our position. It's this president. It's this…. agenda. It has to be stopped, and if we take a stand now, we might have a chance."

Sperling's cell phone rang. He glanced down at the caller ID and picked it up off his desk. "Would you excuse me a moment?" He asked politely and stepped into the hall.

While he was gone, Dianne looked around his office at the shelves full of law books, his college diplomas and photos of Colorado hanging on the walls, and the trinkets on his desk. There was a business card holder, clearly an art project from a young child, a pen-set one with a Colorado flag and one with a United States flag, and there was a ring. At first glance, it appeared to be a class ring, so Dianne had not paid it much attention. But as she sat waiting, her eyes floating around the room a second time, she inspected it more closely.

She pulled out her phone, opened a browser tab, and entered a few words into an image search. The images that came back matched the ring in front of her exactly. The ring was a symbol of leadership within The Order.

"Sorry to keep you waiting," the man said, coming back into the room. "I'm afraid we must wrap this up quicker than I'd hoped. Why don't you work on some cities to target, environmentally progressive population centers, college towns. You know the kind. See if you can scare up some notables. There's always a celebrity who wants his or her name in the paper. I'll send some names as well." He ushered her politely out the door, shaking her hand and said, "I'll be in touch. Enjoy D.C.."

Dianne thanked him for his time and left the Capitol.

* * *

Dianne sent Matthew a text to let him know she was finished with her meeting. He replied he was as well, and they agreed to meet near Smithsonian Castle. It was a more or less halfway point between their locations, and it was a place Matthew had always wanted to see. It was the researcher in him.

Matthew was sitting on the lawn staring up at the building, holding out a foil-wrapped sandwich when Dianne approached. "A lot of food trucks around here," he said. "I took the liberty of getting us some lunch. How did it go?"

"I think it went well. He kind of wrapped it up in a hurry after he got a phone call. How did it go with you?"

Matthew had spent the walk across the National Mall asking himself the same question. He wasn't sure how it went. He didn't have answers. He couldn't even say with certainty he'd confirmed Cummings' involvement. He had confirmed the man knew who he was, and that was something. Neither he nor Dianne knew what to make of it.

"I'm sorry you didn't get any answers, Matthew. I really am."

"What's wrong?" He asked. "Something is bothering you."

Dianne set her sandwich down and sighed. "I think I have a problem, Matthew," she said, not looking at him.

"What problem?"

"Well, you know this campaign I'm working on for Sperling is important to me, right?"

"Of course."

"And it's important to him."

"Right."

"It's possible it's also important to The Order."

"What?"

Dianne explained about the ring. Matthew had seen plenty of pictures of them in his various web-searches and knew exactly the kind of ring she was talking about. It looked like a class ring, with an onyx stone. Not every member was given one, though. It was an honor received by members for some significant achievement or other. Matthew wasn't sure what kind of achievement, but he was fairly certain it had to do with leadership.

"Matthew, what if this isn't just an issue Sperling is passionate about, but something he's pushing on behalf of The Order?"

"It has to do with federal lands and national parks, Dianne. It's probably connected to them."

"What I'm saying though is that it's important to me too. I... The Order..."

Matthew nodded solemnly. "I get it. Working on this campaign might mean working for The Order, the organization I'm trying to expose."

"The two might have nothing to do with the other."

"Possible." He agreed. "But not likely."

Dianne replied, "It comes back to the same question. Why does The Order care so much about the parks; not that I'm not happy someone does..."

"And I'm not a damn step closer to knowing," Matthew said.

26

Rick

Rick met with Annie twice more in those first few days. Mostly, they talked about home. Annie spoke, teary-eyed, about her family and Rick talked about current events and pop culture Annie had missed. She never said how long she'd been in the reality she now occupied. There was a furtiveness about her when their conversations strayed that way, but Rick estimated it had to have been close to a decade.

They also shared theories. The officials, the doctors, the security people they came to know were quick to remind them it was all speculation and that their theories were interesting discussions but not to take any of it too seriously. Rick, knowing they were listening to every word between him and Annie, was careful never to say anything that would show his intention to find a way home.

Annie shared what she'd heard in her time in this "other place." She'd been in a group home of sorts. The residents there did what they could to fit in, learning to live a new life in a new place, and mourning the people they'd left behind. Some of them were also trying to find answers.

That wasn't easy when the facility you called home was government-funded and managed. What Annie had been able to put together was the popular theory, assembled from urban legend, folklore, web-searches, and blog posts. It said people on the other side, *their* side; agencies, governments, private companies were covering up disappearances because they didn't want anyone looking into the rifts between worlds. Some posited that Rick and Annie's "homeworld" wanted to get a hold of whatever technology or energy source it was that opened these rifts, and they had to protect their secret until they figured out how to do so.

"Has anyone been able to slip back through?" Rick asked. He'd asked more than once and, though Annie hadn't dodged the question, she never gave him a straightforward answer.

This time her answer was more complete. "I don't honestly know, Rick. I know there are stories of people who have appeared on this side and then disappeared some time later, but that's not the same as them slipping back through to our world. The people who come through like you and I don't have identities, a paper trail... families. Or if they have families, there's already one of them on this side, you know, like a parallel them."

"A parallel them? You mean, there could be another one of me out there, living my life?"

"Living *his* life. This is his home if there is one of you here. It's not like you could take his place," Annie took a deep breath. She was spinning her wedding ring around her finger.

"It's complicated," she continued. "It's easier for a person to get lost in the system here, or to leave without a trace. We aren't exactly 'off the grid.' These people," she waved her hand around the room, "know we're here, but we don't have lives here, a place. Some people, so I'm told anyway, can't handle it and rather than come back here or stay at a group home and get counseling, they lose it. We don't know what happens to them."

"But they could be going home? I mean, missing people do turn up sometimes."

"Yes. Sometimes they do."

For Rick, it was simple. He would head back to the canyon, back into what he knew as the park, and retrace his steps as closely as he could. He would stay in the wilderness as long as he had to, following as close as he could to the paths he'd walked. And he would keep walking, keep searching until "poof" he was back in familiar territory. Eventually, he'd slip back through and, when he was back in his world, he'd find marked trails, campgrounds, and park rangers. He'd find people looking for him, and he'd go home.

Rick didn't share his plan because he knew how it sounded. He knew Annie would try to talk him out of it, and he would not be talked out of it.

The first step was getting out of the facility.

"How long will they keep me here?" Rick asked.

"Hard to tell. They'll keep evaluating you, interviewing you, testing you until they are certain you can handle the outside world. Well, as sure as they can be. You'll also get the 'hush' talk."

"The hush talk?"

"Yeah, it's when one of the doctors and one of the security officers sit you down and explains that sharing your story with the public would bring undue scrutiny and likely get you labeled as a kook. There's some subtext. I don't know if they bring you back here and lock you up or make you disappear more… terminally. All I know is there are others like us in this building I've never met."

"Surely someone has come through to this side who went to the press or tried bringing attention to the situation."

"How seriously would you take those claims?"

Rick thought for a moment before saying, "If a significant number of people approached me together? I think I'd have to take it seriously."

A line creased Annie's brow. She cocked her head and made a thoughtful sound before saying, "I don't know exactly what that would accomplish, and it would take a lot of people, but you make a good point."

27

Change of Plans

Over the next several days, Dianne organized marches in eleven cities in the United States. She had celebrities and other notables scheduled to speak at seven of them and had reached out to several more. She would speak at the Boston march and spent every minute she wasn't on the phone or writing emails preparing her remarks.

It had been a tough series of conversations between her and Matthew. He wasn't comfortable with her "essentially working for The Order," while she couldn't "give up a fight for important environmental issues just because The Order might have something to do with them." There wasn't any question in either of their minds The Order was involved. It was a matter of how and why.

Matthew developed theories, some of them complex, and all of them unverifiable. It was a puzzle, and he didn't have all the pieces, but he thought he might be seeing the picture. He'd learned that any time a member of The Order involved in state or local government had an opportunity to work towards the preservation and protection of park lands they had done so, even when he or she had no other clear interest or history of supporting environmental protections or regulations.

When he dug deeper, he found not only did those public-lands-related protection or conservation bills always pass, but significant amounts of money seemed to appear from political action committees and lobbyists fighting to pass them.

It was no shock to learn these donors usually had connections to The Order. What was surprising, or would have been were it not for the strangeness Matthew discovered in his initial research, was some of the money came from the aerospace, defense, and energy sectors. There was hard-science money and military-industrial money put up to support "green" initiatives whenever park lands were concerned.

"Is it possible," Matthew asked, "That whatever is causing these disappearances has a strategic value?"

"What do you mean?" Dianne asked with an eraser pressed into her lower lip, her speech notes on the coffee table in front of her.

"I mean... I don't know. Either someone understands or is maybe even responsible for the disappearances within the energy, science, or defense worlds or... or they've stumbled onto something they believe has strategic value."

"Like what?"

"The hell if I know. Okay... Think about the squirrel."

"I'd rather not."

"Bear with me. So, the squirrel vanished, right? It appears from somewhere and then disappears there again. That means there is a *there*, right?"

"A there?"

"Yeah. It had to have come from somewhere and when it vanished if had to have gone somewhere. Right?"

"I suppose."

"I've been hung up thinking about the how, but now I'm thinking the where might be a better question."

"How does the squirrel connect to defense contractors and oil companies?"

"Maybe someone in one of those fields saw something like I did, something appear or disappear. Maybe they got curious about the where themselves. Being strategy or even profit-minded, they might wonder how to use this it to their advantage."

Dianne was sitting upright in her chair now. "Go on."

"So, they decide they need to protect the lands where this stuff is happening.

They make them parks, bring them under the protection of the federal government…"

"But then why would the administration propose budgets that eliminated those protections."

"I've been thinking about that too. What if the administration doesn't know? Maybe it's just the members of The Order who know. It might not be a government project, but an Order project, and they use their influence to protect it."

"Matt, that's insane enough it might be true. Do you think there are places like this all over the world then, surely the United States can't it?"

"It's probably not. But it would be like the space race, only in the hands of a private organization and not the government. Who figures it out, who exploits it, who controls it, would potentially be in a position of some power."

Dianne went to the fridge to get them both a beer. She was chewing the inside of her lip, which she always did when she was thinking hard. Matt thought that over the last few days the inside of her lip had to be raw if not bleeding. "So, what does that mean for us?" She asked.

"I don't know. We can't prove any of it, not without cooperation from someone inside The Order."

"That might have been Roger, and he's dead."

"Right," said Matthew.

"Even if we could prove it, what difference would it make? We'd have to do something with that knowledge," Dianne said. "Just verifying it ourselves doesn't actually help anyone. It changes nothing."

"The Order keeps their secrets. People keep disappearing," Matthew said.

"I don't think we can stop people from disappearing."

"Close the parks," Matt said without considering the implications.

"Close the parks?" Dianne asked, incredulous.

"Don't get rid of them. Close them to tourists," Matt said.

"You're the last person I would ever expect to say that."

Matt answered, "I don't know how else you keep people from wandering off into Narnia, Oz, or wherever they end up."

"You arm them with knowledge. You make sure everything The Order knows, the public knows. Once the secret is exposed, the information is in the public's hands and there are a lot more people, a lot of great minds that can work the problem," Dianne suggested.

"Dianne, you sound like you have an idea. I have heard that tone before."

"You keep doing your research, honey. I'm going to do my thing."

* * *

In the 21st Century, campaigns like the one Dianne was organizing begin with social media. Twitter had become the medium of choice since President Obama's first campaign, and it had grown exponentially since then. A person could make a comment, in Dianne's case issue a rallying cry and, with the click of a button, that cry could be shared, re-shared, and broadcast to the world. When combined with a mass email to existing Earth Action supporters and an image campaign on Instagram that highlighted the beauty of America's National Parks and the threats against them, it was likely she could reach a massive audience in a matter of days.

The greatest strength of the social media approach, with a digital campaign of any kind, was also its greatest weakness; anyone can see it. It is impossible to gather a nationwide support network for an important cause secretly.

"Matthew," Dianne said. "As soon as I broadcast these messages, it's out there."

"I know."

"My reputation, this story which is still a theory... it's all out there. People will respond. The Order will respond."

"I know. But what is the alternative? We can't do nothing." Matthew had taken to using his grandfather's walking stick on his bipedal commute to work and, in the last couple days, had it lying around the house where he could absentmindedly rub his thumb across its smooth top, or spin the little timepiece that dangled from the leather cord. It gave him somewhere to focus his excess nervous energy.

"No, we can't," Dianne said, watching her partner worry at the watch.

* * *

Sperling had called Dianne to offer his congratulations on her campaign. He'd also offered to speak at the march in Washington, D.C. which Dianne could not turn down. "Well, he's definitely not distancing himself from this publicly," she said. "He's willing to be in the center of it whether or not the bill passes."

"That's something, anyway. He may feel differently come Monday."

Major press coverage was all but guaranteed. It wasn't necessary to contact national news outlets and convince them to cover the story. They had teams of people who monitored social media, and the response to the March for the Parks messages Earth Action was getting was hard to ignore. It was trending across platforms. Dianne had contacted local news in each city where a march was planned. They would cover the story and, if things went as planned, the larger news media would pick it up from them and rebroadcast it far and wide.

Dianne had driven to Boston early, to coordinate with city police and act as the face of the rally. It hadn't been easy to get all the permits she needed in all the cities she expected to have major turnouts, but Earth Action did things by the book and went out of their way to work with local law enforcement. No police force was ever happy to have a major political rally in their city, but Dianne had found that making friends early could smooth conflicts later.

Matthew rented a car and drove to Waltham to pick up his grandmother. She wanted to attend the rally but was not interested in calling an Uber to get there.

"I hope this goes well for Dianne," she said when she got in the car. "She's becoming something of a public figure, isn't she?"

"She isn't trying to. She's tried to keep the issue the headline and not her, but yeah she is."

"And what is the issue, kiddo?" Rose asked with a sidelong glance from the passenger seat.

"You know. It's about protecting the national parks from budget cuts and keeping energy companies from gaining access to federal lands."

137

"And?" she asked.

"And?"

"And it all seems conveniently timed with this other mess you've been looking into, your trip to Washington, all of it."

Matthew grinned at her. "It does. Doesn't it? Dianne will explain it better than I ever could. You've watched clips of her speeches."

"She's a passionate one."

"I wouldn't want her leading a campaign against me," Matthew replied.

"Are you safe?" Rose asked.

Matthew sighed. "I think so. It's been quiet since we went to D.C.. No one, as far as we know, is expecting what Dianne is going to say today. What happens after... well, hopefully, she will be too much in the public eye for..."

"Right," Grandma Rose said, patting him on the knee. "I'm proud of you, you know."

Matthew looked her in the eyes and smiled, "Thanks, grandma."

She pointed at the walking stick in the back seat and the little timepiece that dangled from it, "He'd have been awfully proud too."

28

March for the Parks

Linda was in New York City. She had been exceptionally anxious about being the face of Earth Action in such an enormous venue. Public speaking was not her specialty. Dianne told her she was better at it than she gave herself credit for, which was true. That had done little to assuage her anxiety. It had taken tempting her with world-class museums, shopping, and the chance to meet a favorite celebrity who was also scheduled to speak to convince her.

It had been important to Dianne that Linda have a large audience because Linda knew more about what was really going on than anyone other than she and Matthew. They had explained all the details to her before leaving New Hampshire, so she truly understood what they needed to do. Matthew told Dianne later it was the chance to 'stick it to the man' and be involved in a clandestine action that really convinced Linda to go, and not Macy's or the Met.

Their speeches were scheduled for the same time so that if one of them got coverage and the other did not, the news would get out at the scheduled time no matter what. They'd coordinated their appearances to coincide with statistically busy social media times. Dianne was good at what she did.

The turnout far exceeded Dianne's original estimates. Crowds thronged at cities all over the United States, both the ones they had planned and ones they had not. The biggest challenge Earth Action had was contacting organizers in as many of those locations as they could to make sure someone had secured permits and that they would stay on message. Dianne wanted nothing happening to distract attention from what she and Linda were going to say.

She climbed the handful of stairs to the top of the dais they'd built and approached the podium. The sea of people around her cheered and waved, pumped their signs in the air, and stomped their feet.

"Hello, Boston!" She yelled into the microphone.

The crowd erupted.

"Thank you all for coming out on this chilly morning to make yourselves seen, to make our voices heard!"

She paused for another cheer. She let her smile fall and addressed the mic with a solemn expression. "As you know, we are here today because the president of these United States has sent a budget to your congress that would drastically cut funding to our national parks."

There was a cacophony of boos.

"Under this bill, federal lands across the nation will lose their protected status. The delicate wildlife, the at-risk species of plants and animals our Park's Service works to conserve would lose their guardians. The beauty of this land and its important ecosystems will be sacrificed for dollars. Parks from Maine to California will be sold to the highest bidder and, worst of all, this president wants to open some of these lands to fossil fuel exploration. The impact of this bill on our environment will be felt for generations. This administration's regressive policies and actions have already moved the clock ahead on the environmental crisis we face."

The crowd exploded. There were cheers for Dianne and Earth Action, boos for the president and his policies, and a general clamor of inspired Bostonians.

"It goes deeper though, my friends."

Matthew took a deep breath and held it a moment. He glanced at Grandma Rose, who reached down and took a hold of his hand.

"There is more to these parks than most of us know. Hundreds of people go missing in them who are never found. Cold cases in federal lands, national parks, in particular, stack up at an alarming rate. I lost a dear friend just a few weeks ago at Zion National Park in Utah."

The crowd was silent.

"What, you must be asking, does this have to do with protecting the environment? The truth is, I don't know for certain, but it has to do with protecting something. There are powers at work in our government, and it may not be the government acting on its own but forces deep within it, who know what is happening to these missing people. There are those in our government, in major national corporations, and private contractors who have a vested interest in whatever is behind these American citizens vanishing. These people want this budget bill defeated, and so I do. If the secret to what is happening to the missing, like my dear friend Rick, is hidden within these parks, then these parks need to remain protected. If these lands are turned over to private industry, what chance do we have of learning what is really going on?"

The voices coming from the crowd were confused. Questions were being shouted out. Some people were drifting away. Signs weren't being thrust into the air with the same intensity. Dianne was losing them. The message had changed, and it wasn't what people had come to hear.

"Call your representative's offices, bombard them with emails, tweets, Facebook posts. We cannot let our parks be sacrificed. We cannot lose these treasured national lands, and we want to know what is happening in them. We want to know what The Order is doing in our parks!"

* * *

"It seems like a bit of a contradictory message though, doesn't it, David?" The NBC anchor asked the Boston correspondent. "She was calling to save the parks while at the same time suggesting they hide secrets, maybe that they hide nefarious goings-on."

"You're right, Michelle. It seems to send mixed messages. It was clear from the scene it confused the crowd when the subject changed. Time will tell what the takeaway is."

"In the meantime, David, what do you make of her claims?"

"Well, as you know The Order has long been at the center of conspiracy claims from the mundane to the outrageous. It's no secret some powerful politicians and business moguls count themselves among its members. But I don't see a connection between The Order and national parks, certainly not a connection that suggests knowledge of the whereabouts of missing people or the reasons they've gone missing."

"I see," said Michelle. "Thank you, David."

"My pleasure, Michelle."

"We have reached out to several members of The Order, but so far there has been no official comment. Meanwhile, we go to democratic representative Dan Sperling from Colorado who is leading the fight in congress against this budget bill. Congressman Sperling, thank you for joining us. What do you make of the remarks made today in Boston and New York?"

"Well, Michelle, I think Dianne Chambers and Linda Thompson made excellent points about the need to preserve these lands. The president doesn't seem to care about natural beauty or the environment. He is clearly more concerned with taking care of his friends in the 1%."

"What about the comments about the people who go missing from these lands?"

"I can't speak to that, Michelle. It was a bizarre turn for the day to take, and I hope it doesn't distract from the importance of the core message. People need to reach out to their representatives and speak out against this budget."

"You are a member of The Order yourself, are you not Congressman Sperling?"

"I am. I've been a proud member of that esteemed organization for many years, but that has nothing to do with what is at stake here. We must defeat this budget. We must protect our public lands."

"In your time within The Order, have you ever encountered anything to do with missing persons?"

"Michelle, I am here to talk about the real problem. If you have questions about what the president is trying to do, its impact on the environment, and the economies of the states where these park lands are located, I am happy to answer them. That is what matters here."

"Are you saying that missing people don't matter, congressman?"

"I'm saying conspiracy theories are damaging and detract from the message. The American people need to stop this president and defeat his budget."

"Thank you for speaking with us, congressman."

"Thank you, Michelle."

29

Sperling

The Democratic Congressman from Colorado had been on several phone calls that evening, both before and after his appearance on CNN. The first few calls were from other congressmen who wanted to know what he was doing, speaking at a march coordinated by a conspiracy nut whose message could have cost them the support they needed to stop the budget.

Then he had a call from a fellow member of The Order who wanted to know how much Dianne knew and to find out if Sperling was aware Dianne's boyfriend had been poking around where he didn't belong. The last call he took was a sternly worded warning that if Dianne wasn't contained, or if her message got traction, Sperling would be held personally responsible. This call came from J.A. Cummings.

His only outgoing call had been to Dianne. "What in the hell are you doing?"

"I'm sorry, congressman. I did everything I promised I would do. Earth Action is not responsible for the remarks made by me or Linda Thompson. Those were our own."

"And why? Why would you risk the cause you were so obviously passionate about to make a stand over some lunatic conspiracy theory?"

"It's not a lunatic theory, congressman. We both know that. I don't know the details, but I suspect you do."

"And how do you think this helps? How do you think this budget and our fight against it tie into this missing persons nonsense?"

"If the parks are protected, whatever secrets you have are also protected. I suspect that's why you and other members of The Order have fought so hard to save them. If we defeat the budget, the parks stay safe only now the public now knows there are secrets we need to investigate. If the budget passes, the lands you are trying to keep secret become private. Your secret is no longer protected, but there is no guarantee that whoever develops the land will cooperate with any public outcry for an investigation."

"So, why not allow the bill to pass and leave the rest out of it?"

"Because the public has a right to know."

"What if your stunt has just cost us the votes we need? What if people think Earth Action, all its supporters, and I are nuts and decided not to back our play? Then it's all for nothing! Your insane boyfriend talked you into this. It wasn't enough that he risked his own career and put his family in danger, but he dragged you and Earth Action, and any good you could have done right down with him. I hope you're proud of the both of you. And Dianne, for your sake, I hope you're finished."

Sperling ended the call. Dianne's heart was thudding in her chest. She hadn't been sure she was doing the right thing, that the risk was worth it, but as soon as the congressman mentioned Matthew and Rose, people he shouldn't know anything about, all doubt evaporated.

* * *

Matthew and Dianne drove Grandma Rose back to Waltham together. Matt didn't have any choice but to stop in and see his parents. Dianne stayed in the car while Matthew went inside. She liked his parents well enough but was not prepared to answer awkward questions or explain herself to anyone just yet.

"We saw Dianne on TV a little while ago," Matthew's mother said. "She looks well these days." His mother was an Olympic champion at avoiding sticky topics.

"I'll tell her you said so," Matt replied with a forced smile.

"What in the hell was she going on about, Matty?" Dad was the yin to his mother's yang.

"You listen to it?" Grandma Rose asked.

"Sure did, but I don't know what I was listening to," Mr. Conrad replied.

"Well, it's exactly what she said, son." Grandma Rose was taking the heat so Matthew didn't have to. She'd done that for years, challenging her son so her grandson was out of the spotlight. "People go missing in these parks all the time, like Matthew's friend Rick. He and Dianne have been looking into it. It seems some people know more than they're telling. Your son and his girlfriend are taking a stand."

"Well, I hope it works out," Mr. Conrad said and walked out of the living room. "Nice to see you, Matthew," he called back over his shoulder.

"Well…" Mrs. Conrad said. "If you're taking a stand, then I'm proud of you. I don't know how your father and I can help, but you let me know if there is anything we can do."

"Thanks. Just… I don't know. If anyone calls and wants to ask questions about Dianne and me, have them call me. Okay?"

"Okay. Love you, Matty. Tell Dianne we'd like to see her next time. Maybe we can all get dinner one of these nights. Wouldn't that be lovely?"

"It would. Love you, mom."

"Love you too, honey."

Matt turned to his grandmother. "Thanks for coming, grandma. It means a lot."

"Wouldn't have missed it. Now you two take care. Make sure and check in with me… with us." She gave her grandson a tight hug, and he thanked her again before heading back out to the driveway where the car was parked in the shadow of a tree, beneath a nearly moonless sky.

"How did it go?" Dianne asked.

"About like you'd assume. Mom thinks you looked nice and wants to have dinner soon."

Dianne chuckled. "And your dad?"

"Thinks we're lunatics."

"Well, he isn't wrong; not about you anyway. Matt, what have I just done?

Does it even make sense?"

"Well, I know the budget thing is important to you. It's important in general, but I think it was the best chance we had of getting the message out. I really hope it didn't cost you too much support. I…"

"I know. We'll wait and see. I know it was the right thing to do. I wasn't sure, but I am now. You heard the call with Sperling. It's… this is terrifying, Matt. It was the right thing, but I could have just torpedoed my career too."

"I'm so sorry," Matthew replied. "I wish I… If I knew another way-"

Dianne took a deep breath and reached out for Matthew's hand. "There will be other campaigns, and if our reputation suffers, Earth Action's reputation I mean, then we reorganize, rename and keep fighting the fight."

Matthew squeezed her hand. "Thank you. I'm still sorry. Have you spoken to Linda?"

"She's holed up in her hotel right now. I told her not to take any calls. She was more than happy to deflect them all to me. She's going home tomorrow."

"Home sounds like a good idea. Want to get something to eat first?"

"Not at all. I just want to get some sleep."

Matt leaned over and kissed her cheek, then pointed the car north and headed back to Dover.

30

Fallout

The "Twittershpere" exploded after Dianne's speech. Google searches for missing persons, national parks, and The Order had boosted those terms into the "trending" category. Whatever the outcome, the story was spreading. When Matt and Dianne got home, Dianne made herself a cup of tea, turned her phone off, put it on the charging pad, pecked Matthew on the cheek, and went to bed.

"Don't stay up too late, honey," she called down the hallway.

"I'll be in shortly," Matthew said. He opened a bottle of Sam Adams and sat on the couch. He couldn't help but be curious about the news coverage. They hadn't listened to more than a few minutes in the car. He flipped on CNN, who was airing a clip of the Sperling interview back-to-back with a clip of Dianne's speech. It was on a late-night, round table news show, and the talking heads were taking their shots at the issue.

There was the CNN host, a Washington political analyst, a presidential adviser who had evidently worked on the budget, and a representative of the Sierra Club. The anchor was trying to steer the discussion towards the missing persons issue and The Order, but the three guests were trying desperately to keep the conversation about the budget.

The analyst and the adviser were towing the president's party line. It was about balancing the budget, fiscal responsibility, and national priorities. The representative from the Sierra Club emphasized the environmental cost of losing park land or protections. A statement he made caught Matthew's attention. "It's interesting how there is no one from Washington here to defend the conservation side of this issue. The panel feels a little imbalanced."

"We reached out to the National Parks Department," the anchor answered. "We were instructed to direct all questions to the deputy secretary of the Department of the Interior, J.A. Cummings. He could not be reached for comment. Now, what about these missing person stories? What is it about the parks that make them such hotbeds for unusual disappearances?"

Matthew flipped the channel, knowing how the panelists would chase one another around the table for the next half-hour and not needing to see it.

Deciding there wasn't anything worth watching on TV, he picked up his phone and started scrolling through his Facebook and Twitter feeds. There were lots of messages from mutual friends of his and Dianne, including one from Martha.

That morning, Matthew had tried to explain to her what would happen at the march. She hadn't seemed to understand right away, and Matthew couldn't blame her. There was no simple, sane-sounding way to describe what they'd uncovered, but he wanted to prepare Martha for what she was going to hear. Having seen the speech on television, she had more questions. Matt resolved to call her in the morning.

He clicked on a video clip posted by his favorite nighttime talk show host. The video caption was "This Weekend in America." The comedian began, "Tens of thousands of people rallied around the country today to stand against the president's proposed budget cuts, which would take a sizable bite out of our public parks system. And apparently, we need those parks intact because that's where the shadowy, secret cabal makes people disappear with the help of reptilians dressed as park rangers and Smoky the Bear."

Matt rolled his eyes and leaned back into the couch, tossing his phone onto the cushion next to him.

* * *

Matthew had fallen asleep on the couch. It was unusual for him; typically only happening if he'd had a little too much to drink or was good and ill. Neither had been the case, so he was a little disoriented when he came to. He tried to prop himself up straighter, but a knot of muscle on the left side of his neck was punishing him for not sleeping properly, so he remained slumped against the arm of the couch.

When he pried his eyes open and straightened his head, he was even more disoriented. Something was wrong. He couldn't breathe well and couldn't open his mouth at all. Panic shattered the grogginess. Matthew registered he had something stuffed into his mouth and there was a length of tape stretching from cheek to cheek. He could smell the adhesive and tasted soggy cotton and something sharp and bitter. He instinctively tried to reach for it, only to discover he had no use of his hands.

Then he saw Dianne in the same condition, crumpled in the armchair across from him. She had not yet come to. Matt knew she'd gone into the bedroom the night before. There was no way she'd been bound, gagged, and dumped in the chair without waking her up. He'd apparently slept through his own trussing too, and that meant they'd been drugged.

"Ah. Welcome back," a voice said from the kitchen. "I hope you don't mind, but I made myself some coffee. You're almost out of cream, by the way."

Matthew tried to scream.

The voice said, "You know, that's a natural reaction. Everybody does it, even when they know it won't help them. You know you're gagged, but you scream anyway. What's that going to do? I mean, sooner or later it will irritate me, but it will accomplish nothing. In fact, I'm betting one of the reasons you two like this place is its seclusion. Am I right?"

Matt tried saying something through the rag shoved in his mouth, but it only made whatever was in his mouth fall further into the back of his throat, and he started to gag.

A man walked into view. He was stocky, but not of a bodybuilder construction. He wore loose-fitting jeans and had a black thermal shirt beneath a light brown winter coat. His face was kind, a few gentle lines suggesting smiles, not age. Matthew knew without being told his name was Malcolm.

"I was going to wait for your other half to join us Matthew, but it looks like it's just the two of us for now. Let's talk. Well, I'll talk anyway. You see, I really thought having a conversation with your grandma would be enough for you to understand we don't want you poking around, but I should have known you've got that stubborn New England blood in you. It's cool. I respect that. The problem is, it can get you in trouble like you are now."

Dianne had risen through the fog and was going through the same steps Matthew had; confusion, recognition, shock, screaming. Dianne had the advantage of being able to see their abuser and scream in his direction, where Matthew had only been able to see her unconscious form when he opened his eyes. Like Matthew, it only took her a moment of struggling before she realized the futility of it and settled.

After giving her a moment, Malcolm said, "Ah, Dianne. Nice to meet you. You know, you look taller on TV. I'm sorry, I told Matthew I made a pot of coffee and just about dried up your cream. I wish I could share, but I don't know that I can trust you two to keep quiet and you can't enjoy a cup of coffee in your current condition." He waved vaguely at their gags.

Dianne raged and shook against her bonds. Matthew tried to get her to calm back down so she didn't hurt herself, but he couldn't communicate anything effectively. She ran out of strength after only a minute, likely still fighting whatever they'd been drugged with, and slumped.

"Dianne, I was just telling Matthew here how I was surprised he didn't pick up the hint when I took his sweet grandmother for a ride. That Rose is a spunky one. But then I realized its good old-fashioned New England stubbornness that keeps him going. You probably call it 'grit' up here, don't you? Anyway," he turned back to Matthew. "Here's how this will go. I'm going to take the gag out of one of your mouths. You're going to calmly explain to me everything you think you know, followed by how you are going to clean up the mess you've made. If I don't like what I hear, then I'll try the other one. If I still don't like it, we'll have to move on to something else. If I ungag you and you scream or do anything else that complicates our conversation, I'll shoot the other of you in the chest? Does that all seem pretty clear?"

Matthew marveled at how the man's tone was that of someone explaining how to make a grilled cheese sandwich rather than explaining the steps to not get murdered in your own home. He nodded at Malcolm. Dianne pulled at her bonds and tried to yell, tears streaming down her cheeks.

"Matthew, I'll start with you. I am really most interested in what you have to say. No offense," he smiled at Dianne. "And Matthew, if you start screaming, Dianne gets a big old hole in the chest. Then it's just you and me, and I'll still have to pull information out of you. Dianne, that's clear, isn't it?"

Dianne scowled, then rested her chin on her chest, defeated.

"Good! Now, Matthew, the gag is coming out. It will not feel good. That's duct tape, and the rag in your mouth is stuffed in pretty well." He stepped to the couch, leaned over Matt, unceremoniously ripped the tape off his mouth, and yanked out the soggy rag. Matt let out a yelp and a groan but was careful not to shout. "Now, take a few deep breaths and I'll get you a little water. You'll need to wet the whistle since you're going to sing for me. You are going to sing, aren't you?"

31

Like a Bird

Matthew told Malcolm everything that had happened since Rick went missing. He was tiring of repeating the story and was even more tired of repeating himself every time his interrogator wanted to go back over the same ground, but he was given little say in the matter. Occasionally, he would come to a point in the story where Malcolm would turn to Dianne and look for confirmation. She would nod her head and Malcolm would prompt Matthew to continue. Otherwise, Dianne just sat listening, tears streaming down her face.

"Now, that wasn't so hard. Was it?" Malcolm asked.

Matthew shook his head.

"The question now is what to do with you. I really feel for Dianne here. You went poking your nose into things, and she's gotten dragged down with you. Now, I understand you lost a friend, and it's only natural you should want to find answers, but you were warned. You were warned more than once. Your friend Roger tried to tell you. I tried to make a point with little old Rose. You kept going even after you saw a man get killed. Then instead of taking the not-so-subtle hints, you had to go and convince your girlfriend here to open her mouth publicly, which brings a lot of unwanted attention. So, you can see my dilemma. You don't take warnings and I can't have you making all this fuss. My employer will not tolerate the fuss."

"Your employer? You're a member of The Order, I assume."

"Not that it's really your concern, but no. We have a business arrangement. I take care of some things for them, and they take good care of me."

"Does it bother you at all your employer knows something about or is behind unsolved disappearances?"

"Not especially. I'm responsible for a few myself." Malcolm winked at Dianne, smiled at Matthew, and continued, "In fact, that brings us right back to our little dilemma, doesn't it?"

Matthew said nothing. He knew there was nothing he could say to change the outcome Malcolm had already decided on.

Their captor said, "I'll tell you what. I think Dianne would feel a lot better without that gag in her mouth. She could probably use a drink of water too. Don't you think so? You have cooperated with my instructions so far, so I would like to think if I take her gag off, neither of you will start shouting. Will you?"

Dianne and Matthew both shook their heads.

"Good. Now, I want to see if your lovely girlfriend has any ideas about what we should do next." He tore the tape off Dianne's' mouth and removed the rag. She choked and sputtered. There was blood on the rag where she must have bitten her tongue or the inside of her cheek. Malcolm brought her a glass of ice water.

"Nice slow sips. Otherwise, you'll choke." He undid the bonds from her wrists and she took hold of the cup with trembling hands. "So, what do you think we need to do next?"

Dianne licked her lips. She took a couple slow sips, wet her lips again, and asked, "What do you want me to say? What can I say that will change anything?"

"Now see, you mistake my intentions. I really do want to hear what you think needs done. I think there is more than one viable solution here and I'm willing to discuss them. But, if you can't think of anything that will work to the satisfaction of my employer, I will have to rely on the obvious and unpleasant course of action you're probably imagining."

"I could retract my statements," Dianne said, and Matthew stared at her, unsure how to react.

"Go on," Malcolm said.

"I could publicly announce the part of my speech that had to do with the disappearance was a stunt to get media attention."

"Well, that's a start. Do you think it would work?" Malcolm asked.

"I don't know. It might. I could say I was… I don't know that it was a stunt and I had been drinking or I was high."

"Dianne, you can't!" Matthew said.

"Hush now," Malcolm said. "It isn't your turn. Here's the problem with that, little lady. We don't want you completely discredited. Stopping this budget is still important to my employer. We can't undermine your credibility or the cause any more than you already have."

Dianne squeezed her eyes shut. She clenched her jaw and a trickle of tears ran down her cheek. "I could blame Matthew."

Matthew cocked his head to one side and looked at Dianne, his mouth hanging open. She continued, "I could say that my distraught boyfriend talked me into it, that he forced me to do it. We lost a friend, and it broke him. He became raving, desperate. People might be sympathetic. Then I could remind them stopping the budget is what matters and ask their forgiveness for derailing the speeches and shifting the attention."

"That does not clear up Linda Thompson's speech."

"I could say she was doing what I told her to, that I threatened to fire her if she didn't."

"She works for you?"

"Not exactly, but the public doesn't know that."

"And how do you think she'd react to you dashing her reputation more than she's already done herself?"

"She'd get sympathy from people too, from the press. I coerced her into it."

"I wonder if she would tell the same story. I'll have to ask her," Malcolm said.

Dianne's eyes grew suddenly very wide. "You have her? You have Linda?"

"I am not going to answer that, Dianne. I will only ask if it would come as a surprise to you if I did, or that I had a very careful watch on her. Maybe you should assume one or the other to keep everyone safe."

Malcolm paced the room with his hands clasped behind his back. "You discredit yourself, your colleague, your boyfriend, and you redirect attention back where it needs to go. That's a lot of sacrifices."

"Dianne, you can't," Matthew repeated.

"What choice do I have? We're dead otherwise."

Malcolm bobbed his head gently from side to side as if to say 'maybe' or 'probably.'

Matthew turned to Malcolm. "There has to be another way."

"Can you think of one?"

After a moment's silence, Matthew shook his head. Then he suggested, "Maybe we just let the news cycle play out."

"That's a little passive for my tastes, Matthew. I think my employer would agree. It isn't much of a strategy when we're up against the clock. Maybe, if there was more time, but there isn't."

"If I do this," Dianne asked, "what's stopping you from killing us, anyway?"

Malcolm smiled, "Nothing, I suppose. I think if you can fix this, get the attention back where it needs to go, maybe my employer decides you two have successfully learned your lesson and I don't need to come visit again."

* * *

Malcolm removed the rest of their bonds. He let them get up and stretch and even wash their faces and brush the taste of the rags out of their mouths. He suggested they understood the consequences should they try anything problematic for him.

Dianne laid out a plan. She would record a video recanting her comments and post it on YouTube. She'd send the link to every social media platform she was connected to, then email the link to all her Earth Action contacts, the celebrities and politicians who had been involved in the rallies, and anyone else Malcolm thought she should include.

"That sounds like a good place to start," Malcolm said. "You understand, I'll be right here while you do this."

"As long as you're not in the camera frame, that's fine."

Malcolm stepped back a few feet so he was out of the frame of the webcam but still had a clear line of sight to Dianne and her keyboard. He indicated Matthew do the same. Matt pulled up a chair a few feet away and watched Malcolm watch Dianne.

Dianne cleared her throat, brushed her hair out of her face, adjusted the webcam, and hit the record button. "Good afternoon," she said, "This is Dianne Chambers. There is something I need to say to the American people. I am speaking especially to those who have given their time and effort to Earth Action and the resistance movement against this president and his continuing assault on the environment. As I am sure you have heard, I made a speech at a rally in Boston yesterday in which I laid out the reasons stopping the current budget bill is critical. Many other speakers around the nation did the same, most of them more eloquently than I. Having seen the news, I know you probably heard about my speech, and the speech of my colleague and friend Linda Thompson who spoke in New York. You know our speeches went off message."

Dianne took a deep breath and looked at Matthew's reflection in her laptop screen. He nodded slightly, and her expression turned from sorrow and regret to one of steely determination.

"It's worse than that," she said to the camera. Malcolm cocked an eye at her and his expression tightened. "I made remarks about an esteemed organization and their likely involvement in missing persons cases in parks and on federal lands. Well, I am here to tell you," another glance at Matthew in her monitor then she quickly said, "Not only are they involved in whatever's causing these disappearances, but they also hired a man to kill my boyfriend and I. He's here in our home. He drugged and bound us and threatened our lives."

She knew as soon as she said it, Malcolm would be on her.

As soon as her confession took a turn, he lunged, reaching into the pocket of his jacket, likely for a weapon. Matthew was out of his seat, right on his heels, his grandfather's walking stick gripped firmly with both hands. He swung the hardwood branch with all the power, if not technique, of a Red Sox all-star and it connected against the back of Malcolm's head with a startling "thwack."

All this transpired in the time it took Dianne to record the last sentence and hit the upload button on her laptop. It would take a few minutes for it to complete, but once it did it was set to broadcast far and wide.

"Let's go!" She shouted to Matthew. She grabbed her keys off the ring by the door and her cell phone off the coffee table, and they darted out of the apartment.

"Holy shit, Dianne!"

"Holy shit, yourself."

"Is it posted?"

"Not yet. It will take a couple minutes to upload, but as soon as it does I can post it from my phone. I locked the laptop, so Malcolm can't stop the upload when he comes to."

They ran to the car, Dianne fumbling with the keys.

"Where are we going?"

"To check on Linda."

32

Rick

For weeks, Rick demonstrated to the doctors, staff, and security of the facility his calm, cooperative, genial manner. Now, he was finally being transferred to a halfway house. All the interrogations, interviews, psychological analyses, and oaths of silence behind him, Rick 'the man who appeared' Minor could work his plan.

It had taken more than a little convincing, but Annie would join him a few days later. She'd explain to her shrink that Rick had inspired her to want to go back out into the world. Her plan was to try to be placed in the same halfway house as Rick, if possible. If not, they would find one another.

Rick ended up in Salt Lake City. When the security detail who'd loaded him into the car told him their destination, he said, "At least that's a name I recognize. I have some idea where the hell I'm going." A week later, Annie was taken to a home north of Flagstaff, Arizona.

There were no phones in either home, but there were payphones nearby. Residents from each of the houses collected phone numbers from all the others, from people who had traveled between them or carried messages. In fact, to Rick's delight, there was already a bit of an underground communications network used by the "people who appeared."

They used it mostly to keep in touch with one another, to fill each other in on oddities or differences they'd uncovered between the two worlds. Sharing what they'd learned made adapting and blending in easier. Sometimes people on the network used it to locate or ship contraband like burner cellphones. Annie had helped Rick contact some of these people. Tapping into their network hadn't been difficult once he'd gained their trust.

His next move was harder. He asked people to go public. He wanted to coordinate a time when "those who appeared" marched on radio stations, television news studios, and city or town halls. There would not be thousands of them, not like the rallies Dianne organized, but if there were hundreds, even if there were dozens, they would be hard to ignore.

"They watch us, Rick," Annie had cautioned. "They'll stop us one way or another."

"I have to try," he said.

"I know you do."

Rick decided if they came after him, if the reaction of this America's government, law enforcement, or military was to take him out for causing problems, they would have to do it publicly.

"What do I have to lose?" He asked Annie. "This isn't my world. I'm not going to quietly play along pretending it is. Even if no one can figure out how to get me home, at least people will know we exist and maybe look for a way. Maybe people will start demanding answers. It's what Matty and Dianne would do if they were here."

In his first few weeks outside the facility, he'd been in touch with enough people who had nothing to lose, people with a fighting spirit, and people who were simply bored and frustrated, he'd organized something resembling a movement. It had taken him aback just how many people like him there were, and an awful lot of them were tired of their situations.

They coordinated the timing. They organized the rally points. They rehearsed the message. "We don't belong. Help us get home. Your government knows something." Maybe it would be enough and maybe it wouldn't, but if they made sufficient noise, they couldn't be ignored.

33

Linda

Linda didn't answer her phone on the first, second, or third ring. Dianne was more than a little unsettled. Matthew, as they drove at non-standard speeds across Dover and into Durham, had been on the phone with local police.

It occurred to him it was the second time he'd fled the scene of a crime in under a month. "At least it isn't two hours later," he mused. Then, it occurred to him if he was under surveillance, which he would be, his phone number might be flagged or his call routed to the same state police officers who'd responded after the Roger incident. Being caught up in an actual conspiracy made Matthew feel more paranoid than some of the oddballs who ran the conspiracy websites he'd visited.

There was no choice but to explain to the police what had just happened. He told the dispatcher where they were going once they left the apartment and that he wasn't sure how long Malcolm would be out, or if he'd still be there when police arrived. But there would be evidence of what he was telling them.

"Sir, just so I understand, a man you don't know but who recently harassed your grandmother in Waltham, Massachusetts is now in your apartment, unconscious as a result of a head injury you inflicted trying to escape his captivity," the dispatcher summarized.

"Yes. That's about right. I'm sorry it sounds insane, but it's not half as insane as anything else I've been through lately. I suspect my girlfriend and I will not be safe for a while. The people behind this aren't likely to ease up. You know what? Never mind. Just please send officers to the house. We left it unlocked. I will be available on this phone number if they need to contact me. I would like to know if the man is still in our home when they get there. We are going to check on a friend who may also be in danger, and then we'll come into the station."

Matthew shot Dianne a questioning glance, and she nodded her head.

"Thank you, Mr. Conrad. The police are on their way."

"Thank you," Matthew ended the call and said to Dianne, "The police are on their way to the apartment. Dispatcher thinks I'm out of my mind, but they are on their way. Lord only knows what they'll think when they get to the house if Malcolm isn't there."

"You nailed him pretty good."

"Yeah, but… I don't know. He's not a small guy." Matthew looked around the car, tension rising in his shoulders and shooting up his neck. "The walking stick!"

"I think you dropped it in the house when we ran to the car. I'm sure it's at home."

"It's also evidence."

"The police will tag it and, once this is all over, you'll get it back. I'm sorry, Matt."

Matt shook his head. "If Malcolm is gone, there might be blood or something on the stick they can use as evidence."

"Possibly. That's Linda's car," Dianne said as she pulled along the curb outside her friend's house.

"She's still not answering?"

"No. I'm going to go knock on the door. You staying here?"

"I'll come with you." They got out of the car and approached Linda's house. There were a few lights on, but they didn't see anyone moving around. Dianne knocked on the door, but there was no answer. She walked around to a large window on the side of the house that looked into the living room. The TV was on.

"Matt," Dianne called from around the corner. "The TV is on, but I don't see her." She knocked on the glass. Matthew walked around to the other side of the house and stopped when a shout rang from inside.

"What in the actual hell?" Linda called, flipping on the porch light and opening the front door. "You scared the ever-living crap out of me sneaking around in the bushes!"

Dianne ran around to the front door and nearly bowled Linda over on the porch where she stood. Matt came back around front to meet her. "Oh, thank god you're okay. Why weren't you answering your phone?"

"Because the battery is dead, and I was too drunk, then too asleep to put it on the charger. I was asleep on the pot when you psychos started knocking."

Dianne was holding Linda's hand, apologizing and trying to explain why they were so worried about her. Linda wasn't listening. She stared down at her hand and said, "Unauthorized touching," with a playful smirk. She snatched her hand back. "Come in. Tell me all that again, I wasn't listening. It was all very loud and much too fast."

* * *

Dianne filled Linda in on what had happened with Malcolm, Matthew adding detail or clarifying where necessary. It had only taken a few minutes, but they were both breathless by the time they reached the end. Linda listened intently, even as she wandered off to get a glass of water and some aspirin and start the coffeemaker. When they finished the story, Linda asked, "So?"

"So?!" Dianne said, stunned.

"Yeah, so how's the video doing? You trending? You spammed it, right? Is it viral?"

Dianne rubbed her temples and smiled. "I haven't looked yet. I was preoccupied with thinking you were in the hands of a kidnapper assassin hired by a clandestine group of power brokers intent on silencing you."

"Yeah, no, I appreciate that. I'm good. What are your numbers?" Linda was already on her phone, pulling up YouTube. Dianne had her phone out and was looking at analytics on Facebook. The video had uploaded and been successfully shared on Twitter, Facebook, and Instagram. From there it had been shared a handful more times, but it was light years away from viral. Dianne's heart sank.

"It's off traffic hours," Linda consoled. "It will pick up. I mean, it should."

"Unless I have absolutely no credibility and no one cares what I have to say at this point."

"That's possible," Linda agreed, "But I think you're fresh enough in the news cycle to get a little more mileage. I know! If you haven't gotten traction on the video by morning, your new friend Matthew brained will have to be in the paper, the police blotter anyway."

"Unless he's not there," Matthew said.

"If the police respond, it's in the blotter," Linda corrected.

"So?" Dianne asked.

"So, we share the police blotter headline linked to the video. Is there a shot of him coming after you or Matty bashing his brains out?" Matthew grimaced. Dianne nodded. "Then, you're golden. Sleep on it. In the morning, it *will* be trending. I'll help."

"Thanks, Linda. I'm sorry you're mixed up in this."

"Whatever. This is cool as hell. You probably owe me several dinners and bottles of something fancy though. For now, stay here. Get some sleep."

"Thanks," Matt said, "but we have to get to the police station."

34

Yes, Officer

Matthew did the driving to the police station. Driving wasn't his favorite thing, being a walker or bike rider at heart, but Dianne was glued to her phone watching "shares," and "likes," and reading comments. She had ceased her running commentary on the numbers a few minutes into the drive. By the time they'd arrived at the Dover Police Station, her comments had reduced to the occasional milestone update.

"Over a thousand re-tweets."

"1,200 unique hits on YouTube," and the like.

Matthew put the car in park and turned off the engine. Dianne didn't seem to notice.

"Honey, I think they're going to want to talk to both of us."

"Right," she agreed and stowed the phone in her coat pocket.

The meeting with the police sergeant had gone smoother than either Matthew or Dianne had expected. It turned out Malcolm was no longer in the living room when the police arrived, but the gags, zip-tie bonds, and the walking stick spattered with blood were.

"How bloody was it?" Matthew asked. He got a raised eyebrow for this. "Sorry, it's a family…. sentimental… you know."

The sergeant nodded and said, "Then we have this video. It was playing on your computer when officers entered your apartment. I haven't been watching the news, so one of them had to fill me in on the backstory. What interested me was at the end of it you see this man you called Malcolm coming at you, and you can see Mookie Betts here swinging for the green monster."

Officers took statements from Matt and Dianne separately. They were asked a few questions, but nothing that crossed into the territory of The Order, the missing, or any other recent oddities in their lives. As far as the police seemed to be concerned, there had been a home invasion, two people were held captive, and they escaped.

More questions might come up as they investigated and tried to find the assailant, but as far as Dover and New Hampshire State Police were concerned, they were free to return to their apartment and go on about their lives. They assigned an officer to monitor the apartment.

"I know it's not in your jurisdiction, but this man approached other members of my family-"

"Your grandmother? In Waltham?"

"Right. Yeah. I forgot we went over that. So is it possible-"

"I'll make a call to locals down there, and we'll see to it granny and your parents are left well alone."

"Thank you."

"Be safe," the sergeant said and led them out of the precinct to the front desk where he shook their hands and wished them well.

35

Viral

Linda was standing outside the police station when Dianne and Matthew walked out. She was smoking a cigarette and hopping from one foot to the other, thumbing through screens on her phone.

"Linda, what are you doing here?" Dianne asked.

"Oh my god. So, I drove by the house to see if you were there, then when I didn't see you, I remembered you said you had to come here, so I drove over here and I saw your car and I've been waiting for you to come out. Oh my god, Dianne. The numbers!"

Dianne's eyes went wide, and she snatched Linda's phone from her faster than Linda could offer it. With each flick of the thumb, her eyes went wider, and her jaw went slightly slacker.

"I'm assuming it's good," Matthew said, sticking his hands in the pockets of his jacket to ward off the growing chill.

Linda turned to him and said, "Good is when you're sure all your friends and a few of their friends have seen a thing you post. Good is when you have more likes than you have people in your family. Great is the Save the Bay response. Really great is the Protect the Parks March. This... this is something else. This is like-"

"It's like my video has been seen by over a million people. It's emails from several major news organizations and even a message from Stephen Colbert's people."

"That's amazing," Matthew said with a slight tremble in his voice.

"Hell yeah, it is!" Linda agreed.

Dianne handed the phone back to her friend and said to Matt, "What is it?"

"I feel like maybe we aren't out of the woods yet. I'm a little nervous about the scrutiny and attention. How do we know who's connected to what? Surely The Order has news outlets in their pockets. We know they have celebrities in their membership. Maybe they try to trip you up, set you up to fail."

"Colbert is not in The Order," Dianne argued.

"I'm sure you're right and don't misunderstand me. I think it was the right thing to do, besides the fact it probably saved our lives. I'm just nervous."

Linda said, "You mean paranoid, and I get it. But no one will try to touch either of you now. Something happens to you and people will look for whodunit. People will watch this video and ask questions. No, I'd say you're safer now than ever."

Dianne pursed her lips, and Matt ran his fingers through his hair. "I hope you're right," he said.

"Of course I am," Linda replied.

* * *

"President Holds Closed-Door Meeting with Senior DOI Staff Following Viral Video," the headline read. It was one of several headlines popping up in Dianne's social media feeds.

Some were more sensational, "Conspiracy Theorist Posts Cryptic Kidnapping Video," and some were less objective, "Anti-Government Alarmist Again Seeks Media Attention."

Regardless of the language, the irrefutable fact was that Dianne, Matthew, Malcolm, The Order, and the missing were in the news.

In less than twenty-four hours, the story had reached media saturation. People were asking questions.

"Was the video real?"

"What did The Order have to do with kidnapping?"

"What did The Order have to do with the congressional budget hearings?"

"How did either of these things connect to people going missing in national parks?"

Linda stayed glued to Matt and Dianne. It felt safer for all three of them, and they wanted to present a unified message as they rode the wave of telephone calls, emails, and requests for interviews, statements, and public appearances. Matthew had begun the search for the missing, but Dianne had become the face of it. She knew how much to say and when to say it. She knew when to drop a previously undisclosed detail to keep the story hot.

When she added the story of Roger's murder and Grandma Rose's kidnapping, the internet blew up again. Congressmen who were also members of The Order appeared on interview programs and on radio and television regularly. It became impossible for the White House to remain silent on the matter. The first official statement said the president was taking the allegations "very seriously" and would launch an investigation. Congressman Sperling had gone strangely quiet, and J.A. Cummings had been asked to take administrative leave.

Within a week, candlelight vigils in national parks were a regular occurrence, but in addition to mourning the lost, these came with a taste of resistance. It wasn't just families looking for those they had lost. It was people looking for answers and having a direction in which to look.

Several private organizations had filed Freedom of Information Act requests, and there was a general cry from the population for transparency from The Order and the Department of the Interior.

As an organization, The Order had remained silent, but many individuals came forward to confess they knew things were happening within the organization's ranks they didn't want the public to know.

Danielle Riggle appeared on a Sunday morning talk show and admitted she had been in contact with Matthew Conrad when he first began his search. She admitted to having directed him to the Department of the Interior. She told the viewing audience, "The Order is mostly a social club, but there are layers within layers in the ranks and in some of these layers there are secrets and projects they don't want the rest of the membership or the public knowing about. I know for certain one of these projects had to do with national parks."

Her appearance caused another surge in the media storm and before a second week from the posting of Dianne's video passed, scientists, intelligence personnel, military leaders, and PR reps for powerful corporations had been put under the microscope. The public wanted to know what they knew. The public was demanding private investigations of the missing persons cold cases.

Before a month was up, access to specific areas of public lands where people were believed to have gone missing became the sites of investigations. At first, government agencies had tried to keep these investigations quiet and in-house, but the public was not having it.

Matthew, Dianne, Martha, and Grandma Rose traveled to Utah to support a search effort in Zion and the other national parks in Utah. They were not permitted to join the actual search. They hadn't expected to. Matthew felt as though he'd done all the searching he could do. He led a reporter who had tracked him down in Springdale to the area where the ground squirrel had vanished what seemed like a lifetime ago.

"I don't know what it means," Matthew said on camera. "I don't think it gets us any closer to understanding why The Order is keeping secrets, but it was good, solid proof that something abnormal is happening."

"Do you think we will ever find the missing?" the reporter asked.

"I don't know," Matthew said solemnly. "I hope we do. I hope we're able to unravel this enough to find them, or at least get the answers we need from the people who have them. All I know for sure is, as long as we keep looking, as long as we keep asking questions and demanding transparency, even if we can't bring them home, we can bring them some justice."

36

The Nerve

Matthew tried at Zion, but there were too many memories, too much emotional chaos, and there had been far too many people around for him to feel comfortable. When they visited Bryce Canyon, either Grandma Rose or Linda had been by their side. At Arches, Matt convinced Dianne to go for an early evening drive after they met with candlelight vigil goers and protesters. The plan was to stop at a particularly scenic spot and do it before he lost the nerve.

At the Courthouse Towers viewpoint, he fumbled trying to get the box out of his pocket and was too frazzled to go through with it by the time he had. By the Petrified Dunes viewpoint, he'd readjusted the box for easy access but had second-guessed how he would say it, so the box stayed in his pocket.

At Balanced Rock, he decided it was now or never.

Standing with his arm around Dianne, his grandfather's walking stick held tightly in his other hand, he said, "I'm glad we came back here. I know it's been wild. I wasn't sure what to expect from this trip."

"Me either. It's good to see all those people though. They care. They want to be involved and get answers."

Matt sighed, smiled, and said, "And our last trip didn't go exactly as planned."

Dianne smiled and said, "No. I don't suppose it didn't."

"Few things do."

Dianne replied, "That's for sure."

"I'm really sorry it all ended up being such a circus. I had no idea-"

"I'm not sorry, Matt. Sure, I'm a little worried about the future of Earth Action, but who knows? Maybe we learn something about these disappearances. If nothing else, we've helped invigorate interest in the parks."

Matt responded with a nod. "I sincerely appreciate you sticking with me through this. I know it wasn't easy."

"It wasn't. I was pretty sure you were losing your mind."

"I started to think so myself."

There was a long silence as they stood watching the sky turn colors, framing the geological wonders before them. Matthew took a deep breath and ran his fingers through his hair.

"So," Dianne said, "Are you going to ask me?"

Matt choked out, "What?"

"Are you going to ask me?"

"Um... you... I..." was all he managed before giving up, dropping to one knee, and removing the box smoothly from the pocket of his jeans.

"Dianne," he began.

"Of course!" She interrupted. "Yes."

Matthew stood and slid the ring onto her finger, and they shared a deep kiss.

Taking a step back, Dianne said, "I lost the bet, you know."

"What bet?"

"I said we'd be at Canyon Lands before you did this. Your grandma said you'd get up the nerve before we left here."

"You..."

"Yep," Dianne smiled. She took him by the left hand, his right hand wrapped around the walking stick, and they walked back to the car.

37

Epilogue

The movement was much more difficult to keep running than it had been to get it off the ground, Rick was finding. It was easy to get people riled up but without achieving results, it was hard to keep them that way. When arrests started being made and some of the "people who appeared" started getting locked up, support for the movement quickly dwindled.

Conspiracy websites and blogs kept the flame alive, but the public at large never really sunk their teeth into the story. The people who appeared were an urban legend as far as they were concerned. These people showing up in marches and rallies, the ones trying to get on radio talk shows and television were lunatics, fringe conspiracy nuts looking for their fifteen minutes.

Rick knew it was only a matter of time before they came looking for him. He jumped from halfway house to halfway house, using the crude system of relayed messages and off-grid routes been established before his arrival. To some, he was a rabble-rouser. Some of those who had appeared wanted to live as normally as they could and didn't like this newcomer stirring the pot. To others, he was a hero.

Rick recognized he didn't have the skills, the connections, the knowledge of how things worked in his new world to spark any great change, but he knew he was good at convincing people what he wanted them to believe, and as long as there was a secret, as long as people were arriving in one world who'd started in another, he was going to keep them connected and keep them focused on finding answers and maybe one day finding a way back home.

About the Author

I am an elementary school teacher. I have been a paperboy, dishwasher, bookseller, barista, apple picker, customer service manager, rental company manager, flooring installation manager, salesman, retail merchandiser, grocery-warehouse picker, house painter, convenient store clerk, supplement seller, and more.

I have two brothers between whom I am the middle child.

I was born in upstate New York, spent my elementary school years in Pennsylvania, graduated high school in Massachusetts, met my wife while living in Florida, migrated to Tennessee, and have lived in Ohio since 2011.

My first book "Peppermint Lightning" was published in 2014.

I do most of my rough drafting in November as a participant in National Novel Writer's Month. I owe that event my motivation to get started and my wife for the motivation to keep going.

And I'm proudly a big nerd.

You can connect with me on:
- http://peppermintlightning.press
- http://twitter.com/pmintlightning
- http://facebook.com/peppermintlightningpress

Subscribe to my newsletter:

✉ https://landing.mailerlite.com/webforms/landing/m9e1l7

Also by Phillip Davis

Peppermint Lightning

There is a force that powers the Christmas spirit, a magic that makes lights shine brighter, cookies taste sweeter, and keeps reindeer in the air. It is a power as old as Christmas itself, an unseen electric current of kindness, cheer, and good will. That force is called peppermint lightning. It is fading and in need of a champion.Sidney, a nine year old school girl from Pleasant, Ohio, full of peppermint lightning herself, is called upon to help restore that magic to its former glory. She is recruited by a hopeful elf, an English gingerbread man, a matronly reindeer, and a proud snowman to bring the spirit of Christmas, the peppermint lightning, back to a community that has lost theirs. If she fails in her task, the spark of the holiday will fade and with it all the magic of Christmas. Will her determination, her random acts of Christmas kindness, and a little holiday mischief be enough to put the spark back in the season?